Miranda couldn't believe what a mess she'd made of things

"I honestly didn't mean to mislead you," she told Chase. "Do you think we can put this behind us?"

"So we start over as if we'd never met?" he asked.

"Fresh start on Tuesday," she replied, aware that the air above the dock had become charged.

"So today is meaningless," he said. "I forgive you and you forgive me."

Realizing that somehow she'd started down a slippery slope, but not sure where it was leading her, Miranda nodded. "Exactly."

"Seems I need something for which to be forgiven," Chase replied, reaching forward and toppling her into him.

The man can kiss was the last recognizable thought Miranda managed.

Dear Reader,

When I was growing up, my family spent the Fourth of July week on a lake in northwestern Wisconsin, fourteen miles from the town of Rice Lake. The "summer home" belonged to my grandparents, who stayed there from June to early September before retreating to Florida for the winter. Memories of boating, golf, dinner at the country club, lunch on the porch and attending church in a tiny chapel remain some of my favorites to this day.

While the towns and lakes in this book are fictional, the buildings around the lake are based on those I experienced in my childhood. Bringing Chase and Miranda here when I wrote *Bachelor CEO* allowed me to relive some of those good times.

I'm delighted to be part of the MEN MADE IN AMERICA series. Chase McDaniel is definitely an all-American boy. He's determined to claim his birthright as company CEO, although he's not prepared when his grandfather tosses in one last roadblock, in the form of Miranda Craig.

I hope you enjoy reading Chase and Miranda's story as much as I did creating it. Remember, you can always contact me through my Web site at www.micheledunaway.com. Enjoy the romance.

Michele Dunaway

Bachelor CEO

MICHELE DUNAWAY

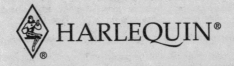

HARLEQUIN®

TORONTO • NEW YORK • LONDON
AMSTERDAM • PARIS • SYDNEY • HAMBURG
STOCKHOLM • ATHENS • TOKYO • MILAN • MADRID
PRAGUE • WARSAW • BUDAPEST • AUCKLAND

Recycling programs
for this product may
not exist in your area.

ISBN-13: 978-0-373-75269-0

BACHELOR CEO

www.eHarlequin.com

Printed in U.S.A.

ABOUT THE AUTHOR

In first grade Michele Dunaway knew she wanted to be a teacher when she grew up, and by second grade she knew she wanted to be an author. By third grade she was determined to be both, and before her high school class reunion, she'd succeeded. In addition to writing romance, Michele is a nationally recognized English and journalism educator who also advises both the yearbook and newspaper at her school. Born and raised in a west county suburb of St. Louis, Missouri, Michele has traveled extensively, with the cities and places she's visited often becoming settings for her stories. Described as a woman who does too much but doesn't ever want to stop, Michele gardens five acres in her spare time and shares her house with two tween daughters and six extremely lazy house cats that rule the roost.

Books by Michele Dunaway

This book is dedicated in memory of all
my grandparents. You helped shape my life
and your love made me a better person.

And thanks to all the teachers in the Francis Howell
High School English department who bought
charity raffle tickets and stacked the odds to give
Mike Storm his supporting role. Mike, for putting up
with me next door in A115 for six years,
this Iowa book is for you.

Chapter One

She shouldn't be bending over like that.

As he gazed at the woman wearing the short blue pinstripe skirt ahead of him, Chase McDaniel's throat constricted and his silk tie suddenly felt tight. She leaned over farther, continuing to study the back end of her car.

He had a perfect view of well-shaped legs that led upward toward…

The bead of sweat that formed on Chase's forehead had nothing to do with the late May heat wave. It might be ninety-two degrees, but the vision in front of him was what was getting him all hot and bothered in the company parking lot this Friday morning.

She straightened, and he noticed how her crisp white shirt clung to her breasts, outlining the white cami she wore beneath. She'd shed the suit coat, and her sunglasses were perched atop her head to keep her short black hair back.

She was hot. Both literally and physically. He'd never seen a woman quite like her, Chase decided. She had a commanding yet sexy presence. His libido heightened, and he worked to control his physical reaction.

Her car was in a visitor space, and as he approached he could see what vexed her—a flat tire.

It was 10:00 a.m., and the official start of the Memorial Day weekend was hours away. Here in Chenille, Iowa, the day promised to be a scorcher. But the unseasonably warm weather was ideal for heating lake water and making the weekend perfect for outdoor activities.

Chase's grandfather was already at the family summer home in Minnesota, and that's where Chase was heading next, once he stopped and did his good deed for the day. "Hi," he said, pausing a few feet from her.

She turned, and he inhaled. She had the greenest eyes he'd ever seen.

"Hi," she replied. Her frustration with the situation was obvious.

"Looks like you have a flat."

"You think?" She rubbed her forehead, and dirt from the tire streaked her skin. His fingers itched to wipe the smudge off, but he kept his hands to himself. He'd liked her on sight, and being up close hadn't done anything to change his mind.

"Do you know of a repair shop I can call?" she asked, focusing on the matter at hand.

"Do you have a spare?" Chase countered.

She wrinkled her nose. "I hope so. I've never had to use it. Never even looked to see if it's there."

He moved to her trunk and noticed her Illinois license plates. Chenille was an hour northwest of Dubuque, which sat on the Iowa-Illinois-Wisconsin border. "Where are you from?"

"Chicago," she replied, watching as he lifted the trunk lid. "What are you doing?"

"Changing your tire." Chase gave her the grin that

his sister Chandy declared irresistible. "You're in Iowa. We do things like that, especially out here in Chenille."

"I'd never even heard of this town until a few weeks ago," she admitted. "Couldn't have found it on a map before then either."

He laughed. "Not many people can unless you're looking for us. We're a company town owing our livelihoods to McDaniel Manufacturing. I assume since you're here you've heard of the products."

"Oh, I dug around a little. McDaniel Manufacturing makes cheeses, ice cream and other assorted dairy items. The popular product lines give Kraft a solid run for their money."

He tossed her trunk mat on the ground, wondering about the purpose of her visit. She'd driven a long way. Maybe she was in sales. A lot of vendors and suppliers did come calling. "So you did your research."

"Any smart woman would."

"And you're a smart woman?" He refrained from adding that if she was, she'd have checked her trunk for a tire. Luckily, she had one, and it was inflated.

"I like to think so."

Chase chuckled, unscrewing the bolt that held her tire jack and spare in place. "So where'd you go to school?"

"Northwestern University."

"Good old Evanston," he said, placing the bolt in his pants pocket. He didn't want to lose that.

She took his words the wrong way. "Do you have a problem with Northwestern?"

"Nope. Not if you don't care that I went to the University of Iowa," he replied. He removed the car's jack and handed it to her. His fingers brushed hers for a second as she took it from him.

After placing the spare on the ground, he shed his suit coat and rolled up his sleeves. He'd never been afraid of dirt or hard work, and he could shower when he reached Lone Pine Lake.

He'd be about a half hour late, but his grandfather would understand. Leroy was all about chivalry, especially on the parking lot of the company he owned and loved.

Chase loosened the lug nuts and he placed the jack under the frame of the car. He inserted the handle and began to turn it, raising the car up slowly until the tire was free of the ground.

Then he removed the lug nuts and the bad tire, ignoring that his hands had turned black from the brake dust and the road grime. He slid the spare on, reversed the process, and soon had her car ready to go.

"Thank you."

"No problem." He put the flat in the trunk and set everything on top. "If I were you, I'd take this down to Bay's Tire and have them look at it. Bay's is right there on the main drag. You can't miss it. Looks like an old gas station without the pumps. Tell them Chase sent you."

"Okay." She crossed her arms over her chest and studied him.

"So, where are you heading after this? Going inside?" he asked.

She shook her head, her short locks swishing. "No. I'm finished. I'm actually starting work here Tuesday. I filled out my tax forms today."

"Oh." He frowned. Come Tuesday she'd be an employee. Chase had been well schooled in sexual harassment law. McDaniel Manufacturing prided itself on its employee satisfaction, stellar work environment and safety record.

Still, she wasn't quite on the job yet, and something about her intrigued him. Curious to learn more, he said, "I was wondering if you'd like to reward me for my valor by letting me take you to an early lunch."

Instead of saying yes, she arched a dark eyebrow and her pixie mouth formed a slight pucker. "That's sweet, and I really appreciate your offer, but you've already helped me out enough. I should have joined an auto club or something. As it is, I've got to get going. The moving van is on its way, if it's not already waiting at my apartment."

"They're always late," he replied, delaying her inevitable departure. Of course, he really had no clue about moving companies. He'd only moved once, from his grandfather's estate to his own place, ten years ago.

However, she was already edging away, to the driver's side of the car. He stood there feeling like a fool. "It was nice meeting you," he said.

"Thank you again," she replied.

"You're welcome." Chase remained frozen in place until she drove off. Then he retrieved the suit coat he'd set on the ground. His dry cleaners would kill him, but the bill would be well worth it.

Chenille had never seen anything like her.

If it had, Chase would have found her long ago. Goodness knows he'd gone through enough women looking for the right one. Sex was never an issue. The problem was finding someone who could keep his mind and heart interested, as well. Someone he could love forever. Call him a closet romantic, but he believed in true love and wouldn't settle until he found it.

He held up his dirty hands and grimaced. Even though he'd brought his suitcase with him, it might be best if he went home to shower before leaving for Minnesota. He should be able to do so and still be in plenty of time. His grandfather had specifically asked him to arrive earlier than the rest of his siblings. Every Memorial Day weekend the entire family gathered at the house on Lone Pine Lake, starting Friday night, to kick off the summer and celebrate Leroy's birthday.

His grandfather would be eighty tomorrow, and Chase was certain Leroy was finally ready to announce his retirement. He'd been hinting for a while about passing the torch. Chase had been groomed his whole life to become CEO of the family business, a role and legacy that had passed to him when his parents died in a single-engine-plane crash.

Once he'd had dreams of leaving Chenille and making his way in some big city, but he'd long ago left those fantasies to his siblings.

His sister Cecilia had made her home in New York as a professional ballerina. Now thirty and at the end of her dancing career, she'd started teaching ballet, gotten married and had a child on the way. Chase's younger brother, Chris, was also married, and worked in Davenport as a minister. The youngest of the McDaniel clan, twenty-seven-year old Chandy, was doing her pediatric residency in Saint Louis.

Chase drove the short distance to his home, an atrium ranch sitting on five acres. He'd hoped to share it with a wife and kids, but he refused to get married until he knew he'd found his soul mate. Everyone in his family had happy marriages, and Chase wanted the same.

For a second, he thought of the woman he'd met. McDaniel currently had several management openings, two in human resources. Maybe she'd filled one of those.

He washed his hands and resisted the urge to call the office, especially since it was a holiday weekend and he'd told his secretary to take the rest of the day off. Tuesday morning would arrive soon enough. Surely he could find out who the mystery woman was then.

MIRANDA CRAIG FOUND Bay Tire easily, and within a few minutes was sitting inside the store, watching while a cat yawned his assessment and sauntered off.

Her tire couldn't be plugged, so she nodded in approval of the new one they wanted to install.

This wasn't one of those chain establishments, but rather a mom-and-pop operation. "So Chase sent you?" the wife asked, flipping through a magazine while her husband changed the tire. Both seemed to be in their early fifties.

"He did," Miranda replied.

"His whole family buys their tires here. Have for years. You his girlfriend?" Mrs. Bay set her magazine down for a minute.

Miranda shook her head. "No. I'm a new employee."

The woman gave her a once-over, and Miranda squirmed. "Probably for the best. He does seem to go through women like water."

"Uh-huh." Miranda was grateful when Mrs. Bay began reading an article. It was easy to understand why women would be attracted to Chase. Miranda had felt that initial quiver of interest herself, before she'd realized exactly who the tall blond guy approaching her was. Chase McDaniel wasn't quite the boy next door.

He was a lot hotter and a lot sexier than he looked in the photos she'd seen on the Internet. His pictures had done him justice, but came nowhere close to capturing the man in the flesh.

His hair was sandy-blond, like something you might find on a California surfer. His ocean-blue eyes had sparkled, and his mouth… To be kissed by those full sensuous lips could only be heavenly.

His dress shirt hadn't hidden the fact that he was fit and toned, and the thought of touching his six-pack abs sent chills down her spine.

He hadn't bothered to conceal his interest. His attentions had flattered her, as had his willingness to get his hands dirty. He wasn't such a pretty boy that he was afraid of grease and grime. She'd found him highly attractive and extremely tempting.

She'd wanted to say yes to his offer of lunch, but no was the safer choice, and Miranda always erred on the side of safety. At thirty-three, she'd given up everything in Chicago and had to make a success of her new life in Chenille.

Flirting with Chase McDaniel, thirty-five-year-old heir to the McDaniel Manufacturing throne, would only complicate matters.

She couldn't let his cheeky grin sway her from her destiny. She'd made that mistake before. She'd fallen fast and hard for Manuel, a dark-haired smooth talker. Eventually she'd figured out his seduction wasn't about her, but about what he could get from her company. She'd discovered that he was using her to win a big contract between her firm and his. The knowledge he'd lied to her and hadn't truly cared for her at all had wounded her deeply.

"You're all done," Mr. Bay said, reentering the shop. He wiped his hands, reminding Miranda of Chase. "You're good to go."

Miranda dispelled the image of Chase's smile. No need for her knees to wobble. She had a long weekend ahead of her, and unfortunately, she'd be seeing him again soon. Tomorrow, in fact.

The reality was he was a means to her dream job, and she wasn't going to let her physical attraction to the man stand in the way of finally getting what she wanted—a chance to shatter the glass ceiling. She'd come too far to fail now, no matter how much he'd piqued her interest.

Cursing under her breath at how unfair life was, Miranda went to pay her bill.

THE MCDANIEL LODGE on Lone Pine Lake had been in the family since the mid-1950s, when Leroy had purchased the property on a rare whim.

As Chase climbed the back stairs, he realized that someday, this too would be his. He paused, his hand resting on the cedar railing while he took a minute to gaze past the house to the shoreline.

Chase had been spending summers at Lone Pine Lake ever since he'd been born, and whatever stress he was feeling always disappeared the minute he stepped out of his car.

He could understand why his grandfather loved the lodge and why he spent most of the workweek here from Memorial Day to Labor Day. The lodge was like fine wine; it developed more character as it aged. The house sprawled at the top of a grassy knoll and offered a panoramic view of the four hundred feet of shoreline at the front of the property.

The entire estate consisted of ten acres, and besides the lodge, two small guest cottages sat a short distance away. The lodge itself had five bedrooms and slept fourteen. The cottages each slept four.

Chase inhaled, letting his lungs and senses fill up

with the earthen smells of crisp air and fresh pine. An eagle soared across the water, talons out as it descended to catch a fish. Lone Pine Lake, with its fourteen miles of shoreline, remained an untouched gem. The houses surrounding the McDaniel estate also sat on acreage, and there were no condos or high-rises anywhere on the lake.

He'd always felt at home here, even more so than at his grandfather's massive residence in Chenille, where Chase and his siblings had grown up.

"You going to stand there all day?"

"Hey, Grandpa," Chase said as Leroy came around the side of the house with a fishing pole in one hand and a tackle box in the other. There was a boathouse near the dock, but Leroy liked to keep his gear on the screened-in back porch. "Was the fishing any good?"

"Nah. Still can't convince me that there are any fish in this lake," Leroy replied with a snort.

Chase laughed. The largest fish his grandfather had ever pulled from Lone Pine wasn't even close to being a keeper. It was the family joke that the fish knew when a McDaniel lure was in the water.

"I expected you a little while ago. You didn't have any trouble, did you?" Leroy asked, thumping up the stairs, pole in hand.

"No." Chase stepped aside to let him pass. His grandfather was six inches shorter than Chase, and slowly shrinking with age.

Chase waited while Leroy put away his fishing gear, and then followed him into the spacious kitchen. Decades ago the house had been a hunting lodge, where a cook had prepared meals for many. The room's most recent updating had been about eight years ago, three years before Chase's grandmother's death. His grandfather had little use for the gleaming stainless steel appliances, preferring to simply microwave some soup or a frozen meal when he wasn't eating out. The local country club was open to the public and had the best food in the area.

Leroy reached into the big SubZero refrigerator and removed a pitcher of iced tea. "Grab me a glass, will you?"

"Sure." Chase opened a cabinet and took out two tall tumblers. Because he hadn't stopped on the drive up he was hungry and thirsty. "So what did you want me to come up early for?"

"Did you bring all my work from the office?" Leroy asked, after taking a sip.

"Everything your secretary gave me," Chase replied, balancing his own glass. "It's out in my trunk with my luggage."

"That's fine. I'm going to go wash up. Let's meet in twenty minutes."

"Perfect. I want to unpack and make a sandwich. I missed lunch."

"Okay." Glass in hand, Leroy left the room. Chase drained his iced tea, put the tumbler in the dishwasher and made a turkey sandwich. When finished, he retrieved his cases from the car.

This was his first visit since closing the house last fall, and as he carried everything in, he looked to see if there were any changes from last year. He wandered through the kitchen and entered the huge vaulted great room.

He set the big envelope Leroy's secretary had given him on the dining room table, and paused to take in the view of the water through the front windows. To Chase's right was a glassed-in porch that could easily seat forty people when filled with tables.

The great room contained multiple groupings of comfortable sofas and armchairs, beneath a ceiling that rose to twenty-five feet. The bedrooms were located in a wing on the far end of the house, opposite the enclosed sunporch.

Chase made his way to his bedroom, on the second floor. He unpacked before returning to the great room and curling up in his favorite armchair near the floor-to-ceiling fireplace. He had fond memories of crackling fires that heated the pinkish-colored stones until they were hot to the touch.

"Ah, good, you're here," his grandfather said, emerging from the first-floor hallway that led to the master bedroom and Leroy's office.

"I put your stuff on the table," Chase said.

"I'll look at everything later. Are you still hungry? I thought we could swing over to the country club for a quick appetizer and a drink before everyone gets here."

"I'm fine," Chase answered. It wasn't yet 4:00 p.m. His siblings would start arriving around five-thirty. "You said you needed to talk to me," he prodded, a bit surprised by his urgency to hear the official word that he'd be CEO. He'd always assumed there'd be no glitches, but now that the time had arrived, he was a little nervous. He simply wanted everything signed, sealed and delivered, so he could relax and enjoy the weekend festivities.

Leroy settled into his recliner and kicked up his feet. While he might appear relaxed, his blue eyes were razor sharp and his gaze locked on to Chase. "I'm worried about you," he stated.

"W-why?" Chase sputtered in surprise. The last time his grandfather had been worried, Chase had been seventeen and had failed to call and say that he'd be late arriving home one night. "What are you worried about? Have I made a mistake of some sort?"

"No, no, it's me who's screwed up." His grandfather exhaled a sigh.

"You're not ill, are you?"

Leroy produced a reassuring smile, and with a slight shake of his head said, "It's nothing like that. I'm fit as a fiddle. Unlike my Heidi, I've got quite a few years left in me. Someone has to be there for the grandkids your dad and mom never got to enjoy."

Chase frowned. He knew his grandfather missed his wife and son, but he'd never seen the old man like this. He seemed vulnerable. He never revealed weakness.

Leroy was a tough, self-made man. He didn't crack under pressure. But he appeared to be doing so now. He'd become nostalgic and reminiscent. Maybe that occurred when you hit eighty. Chase didn't know.

The only thing he was certain of was that his stomach had become unsettled, the turkey sitting like a lead weight. Something was wrong. He sensed a problem, knew it instinctively, as he had that day long ago when his grandparents had come to tell him his mother and father were dead.

The knowledge that whatever this was couldn't be as severe as that announcement didn't necessarily provide comfort.

Leroy sighed. "I've been unfair to you, Chase. I realized that a few months ago. You've always done everything I've asked of you."

"It's been no problem," Chase assured him. "I haven't minded."

Leroy exhaled again, as if the conversation pained him. He shifted, lowering the footrest and leaning forward to plant both feet on the floor. He clasped his hands together. "Yes, it is a problem. One I should have stopped long ago. You should have had the freedom to make your own choices. You've been trapped into an endless cycle of meeting my expectations."

Chase's forehead creased. "You've lost me. I don't meet your expectations?"

"Of course you do. You exceed them, actually. No grandfather could be prouder."

"So what's this about?"

"I've spent the last few months contemplating my mortality. I've always said I'd step down when I hit eighty, but I've had a change of heart. I think I'll stay another year."

"Well, that's great," Chase said, fumbling for the correct words. So that's all this was about. Leroy was afraid Chase would be disappointed at not being named CEO.

"I wanted to tell you first. I know I've been grooming you to take over for me, but…" Leroy's voice trailed off.

"It's fine," Chase said quickly. "Another year is no big deal. I'm actually glad you're staying. Work's kept you young. You'd miss it too much."

"It's certainly kept me busy, and that keeps my mind off other things," Leroy corrected. One corner of his lips inched upward in a sad, reflective smile. "No, this isn't about me. It's about you, and my failure to do what's right. I'm not sure being CEO is what's best for you."

"What?" The word shot out of Chase's mouth, propelled by pure shock. "You're kidding."

"No, I'm not. I've come to realize that you've always been expected to work for me at McDaniel. I've groomed you to fill your father's shoes, without really asking if that's what you wanted. Remember when you wanted to be a forest ranger? Or a doctor?"

"That's Chris and Chandy. If I considered medicine, it was a long time ago. I almost passed out after the last company blood drive."

Chase's head was spinning. He felt as if he'd been sideswiped. "I love working at McDaniel Manufacturing. I've never resented it. I'm happy there."

"Still, I've never given you the opportunity to explore other options. When your father died I assumed you would take his place in the business. I should have given you the freedom to choose your career, like your brother and sisters."

"I chose business," Chase protested. "I have an MBA."

"Only because I expected you to get one," his grandfather pointed out, unclasping his hands and gripping his knees. "You've always done what was expected of you. Life's too short to live that way. I want you to break the rules. Go forth and have some fun. Sail the seven seas. Hike Everest. See if there's another career calling your name. I want you to be happy."

"I am happy," Chase said, as the hopelessness of the situation became clear. His grandfather had made up his mind. He'd determined that he'd failed Chase, which meant he was immovable. Leroy was known for not backing down once he'd decided on a course of action.

"I want you to be sure. I'm giving you the next year off with pay. If you decide McDaniel is where you want to be, this time next summer I'll step aside and you'll fill my shoes as CEO, no questions asked. But I believe you need time to think. To be really sure your heart is into running the company I built."

"Of course it is," Chase insisted.

His grandfather conceded with a tilt of his head. "You say that now, but that's because you've never been truly allowed to make your own decisions. Don't worry about disappointing me. I'd be more upset if you didn't take this time to reflect and find out what's right for Chase, not what's right for McDaniel."

"But all the work I do…"

"You aren't indispensable. It can be handled. We have plenty of people who can cover for you." Leroy leaned back and kicked his feet up again. "You know, I wish I'd had this opportunity. At twenty I was already running the family farm. Then I started expanding and producing, and your father was born two years after Heidi and I married. Don't get me wrong. I loved every minute. I just want you to be sure."

"I am." Darn Leroy for not seeing that!

Chase wondered if his grandfather might be experiencing the onset of some kind of dementia. That would explain this sudden irrationality.

The older man smiled and got back to business. "You'll have a year to explore what you want to do with your life."

"Fine," he snapped. His grandfather wanted to give him this opportunity. Chase had no desire to take it, but he had no choice. "In one year I'll be back here and you'll be stepping aside," he declared.

"I admire your spunk. You remind me of myself at your age. We'll see if it's still what you want by the end of the year. If it's really what you want, I'll step aside, as I said, with no questions asked," Leroy promised.

They fell silent, each lost in thought as they watched a pontoon boat motor by. His grandfather's announcement had thrown Chase for a loop. He'd expected to be named CEO, not handed a one-year time-out. He'd been banished from the kingdom, so to speak.

"So where will you go first?" Leroy asked.

Chase frowned. That was the worst part of this mandatory sabbatical. His life had always been mapped out. Go to college. Go to work. Become CEO. Now he'd been set adrift. He answered honestly, "I have absolutely no idea."

Chapter Two

Miranda checked the road map again, trying to figure out where she was. Getting from Chenille to Lone Pine Lake did not involve an interstate, and for the last several miles she'd been looking for Highway A, which according to her directions was just past a big red barn.

So far she'd seen neither barn nor road, and she wished she'd splurged and bought one of those GPS navigators. Since she mostly took the train or the El in Chicago, she hadn't realized how useful a GPS would be.

As it was, she was a little hesitant about attending today's birthday bash. But Mr. McDaniel—Leroy, she amended; he'd insisted she call him that—had wanted her to be there for some big announcement he planned to make.

She rubbed the bridge of her nose and readjusted her sunglasses. She hated being the center of attention, and prayed the announcement wasn't about her. She knew she'd have to get accustomed to the spotlight, especially given her new position.

But that didn't mean she had to enjoy it. She'd always been a private person, never wanting others to know she wasn't quite like them. They'd known, though. In high school they'd looked down on her, called her names behind her back. In college she'd stayed out of the social scene.

Miranda squinted behind her shades, thinking she saw a big red barn looming ahead.

AFTER LUNCH WITH HIS grandfather and siblings, Chase paced the enclosed sunporch. Normally everyone retired for a siesta, but Chase had asked to talk with his brother and sisters.

"You have to help me change his mind. Please."

"Maybe this will be a good thing for you," Cecilia mused. She rubbed her stomach, her belly protruding with the baby due at the beginning of August.

"How can this be good?" Even after sleeping on his grandfather's decision, Chase had woken up not liking it one bit. "He's supposed to be retiring. He's eighty today."

"We know. We all sang happy birthday first thing this morning," Chandy soothed.

"He's not going to live forever," Chase protested.

"And you have plenty of life left. He's told you you'll be CEO if you want. It's only for one year," Chris pointed out. His brother was the compromiser in the family, always looking for the silver lining.

"Grandpa never breaks a promise. Remember when I asked for horseback lessons? It took awhile but he didn't forget," Chandy said.

She'd been a toddler when their parents died, so Leroy was really the only parent she'd ever known. The youngest, Chandy had been raised like a little princess, with Leroy her hero. Because of that, Chase's sister was blind to their grandfather's flaws.

"This isn't like that. He's feeling guilty. He thinks he's held me back from achieving my dreams, from doing the things you all did. He wants me to have a choice about being CEO, but that's not necessary."

"For some reason he thinks it is," Chris said.

"But why now? I'm ready. I don't need to go find myself."

"Have you told him that?" Cecilia asked.

Chase dragged a hand through his hair. "Yes. But you know how stubborn he is once he's made up his mind."

"Well, it's what Grandpa wants for you," Chris replied pragmatically. He was smaller than his brother, topping out at five foot ten inches, but he had similar features. All the McDaniel children did. Blond hair was predominant and they all had blue eyes.

"Well, *I* want to be CEO. That's why I need your help," Chase tried to explain.

His siblings couldn't understand, he suddenly realized. They'd moved out, moved elsewhere. They flew home for major holidays and family events. They phoned, e-mailed and sent cards.

Only Chase had remained in Chenille. He'd stepped into their father's shoes and the life their father had loved. Chase had considered it an honor to have such a duty, and he'd thrived. He'd met every expectation, aside from finding a wife and having a bunch of kids. Chris had taken care of that, and Cecilia would next.

His sister reached out and put a slim hand on his arm. She'd always been tall and graceful, and even pregnant, her dancer's body remained svelte and lean, but with a baby bump. "We can see that you're upset. We're not against you on this. We love you and we'll see what we can do. We'll all talk to him, although like you said, it probably won't do any good. But we'll try."

"Thank you," Chase said.

His sister nodded at the others. "We owe it to Chase."

"Grandpa only wants to help," Chandy insisted.

"Yes, but he may have misread the situation," Cecilia replied.

She glanced through the glass dividing the porch from the great room, where her husband sat reading a book. "The guests should be arriving for the festivities sometime after four. I suggest we let Grandpa have his nap, and talk to him when he wakes up. Hopefully, he'll spare us a minute. Walter is here already, and you know how thick those two are."

"Once the party starts it will be absolutely impossible," Chandy predicted.

"We'll try to get to him before the guests arrive," Cecilia said.

It was the best Chase could ask for. "Thanks."

He looked out the porch windows. On the flat back lawn behind the house, the caterers had set up tents and tables, and were working on food preparation. Over ninety guests were expected.

Most of them would be staying at the nearest motel, or one of the resort cottages in the area. As for the two small guesthouses on the McDaniel estate, their grandmother's sister was living in one for the entire summer; and this weekend Leroy's good friend and business colleague, Walter Peters, would occupy the other. Walter had arrived earlier from Chicago, and like Leroy, was napping.

Chase had never seen the need for a siesta. He'd found that exercise always cleared his mind better than sleep.

His siblings disbanded, leaving the room and returning to other activities. Chase glanced at his watch. He had a few hours before the party started, and no desire to remain inside on such a gorgeous day.

He strode into his bedroom, stripped and donned

his bike shorts and shirt. He grabbed his bike from the screened-in porch, put on his helmet and hit the rural highways. Traffic was light, and he inhaled deeply as the satisfying burn began in his legs.

During the summer he would ride at least twenty miles a day, usually doing seventy-five to a hundred miles one day each weekend. When he wasn't coming to the lake to visit Leroy, Chase would fasten his bike to the rack on the back of his hybrid SUV, throw an overnight bag and a tent in the vehicle and head out for some new place. He was king of the campground.

The lake itself offered diversion, and Chase would often take the catamaran out. They had other watercraft as well, and maybe Sunday, once things died down, he and his siblings could go water-skiing.

Today, Chase decided to do a quick loop through the state park. He'd ride about two miles on Highway A on the return trip before turning onto the last few asphalt side roads leading back to the lodge.

He switched gears and purged his grandfather and the current debacle from his mind, tuning in to his body. For a couple hours, at least, he could be free from stress.

MIRANDA CHECKED THE CLOCK on her dashboard. Even though the birthday party didn't start until four, and Walter had insisted most people wouldn't show until at least five-thirty, she'd been told to arrive before three. She was going to be late.

She pulled over to the shoulder of Highway A. Once she'd found the barn and the road, she'd followed instructions and stayed on the blacktop for fifty miles. Unable to find her next turnoff, she'd driven back and forth over the same five-mile stretch at least three times. She'd finally realized that spotting the elusive road was hopeless, and had been parked for the last ten minutes trying to decide what to do.

Walter had insisted there would be some sort of sign announcing the turnoff to North Shore Drive, but so far she hadn't seen one. In the ten years she'd worked for Walter, she'd never known him to be wrong, which made the mistake hers. She allowed herself a wistful smile. Surely he'd laugh at this foible. Walter had mentored her growth in the cutthroat world of business. He'd once told her that he'd never seen anyone work harder, which was one of the reasons he'd first noticed her and moved her into a fast-track position within the company. He'd said that as a young man he'd received a leg up from the former CEO, and felt honored to carry on the tradition.

He'd made Miranda responsible for millions of dollars and hundreds of employees. She'd proved her competency again and again.

Not that it helped her now. Venting her frustration, she pounded her hands on the steering wheel. She'd already tried her cell phone, but had no service in this neck of the woods.

She'd expected this part of Minnesota to be more like Iowa—miles and miles of open farmland. Instead she'd probably found the last old-growth pine forest in the country. So much for a "lone" pine.

She glanced in her mirror and saw a cyclist approaching. Maybe he could help. Cyclists weren't usually muggers or rapists, right? And if the guy on the bike knew where he was going, maybe he could give her directions. Despite all the warnings to stay safely inside the vehicle with doors and windows locked, Miranda went with her gut, and stepped out of the car.

The cyclist drew to a stop next to her. He was a tall, fit man. His bike shirt clung to six-pack abs. His shoes hit the pavement with a click, and she tried not to stare at his legs. Because of his sunglasses, she couldn't see his eyes—not that she was looking at his face, anyway.

She heard his voice, though—an incredulous demand: "What the hell are you doing here?"

CHASE HAD BEEN ALMOST back home when he'd seen the car on the side of the road. The ride had been invigorating and exactly what he needed. He'd get to the lodge, take a shower and dress for tonight's party, all with time to spare.

He hadn't thought much about the parked car until he'd drawn closer. Then he'd noticed the vehicle was silver, a sensible little four-door sedan…with Illinois plates.

He knew that car. He'd changed its tire. Twice in two days was more than a coincidence.

When its owner stepped from the car he'd enjoyed a glimpse of toned calf muscles under the red capri pants she wore. He'd braked, coming up next to her. And said the first thing that came to mind.

He could tell he'd surprised her, because she drew back slightly, the words of greeting dying on her lips. Man, those lips. They'd tortured him. Not as much as his grandfather's announcement, but close enough to do some damage to his sleep.

"I'm starting to think you're stalking me," he said.

Her hypnotic green eyes widened farther. "Me? I don't even know you."

He reached up and removed his mirrored sunglasses. "We met yesterday." Though he still didn't know her name, he realized. "Remember?"

She exhaled, relieved at seeing him. "Chase. You scared me."

"Do you have something to be afraid of, Ms…." He let his voice trail off.

"Miranda Craig," she offered.

A pretty name, and not one he recognized.

"So what are you doing so far from Chenille, Miranda Craig?" He liked the way her name rolled off his tongue. "Don't you have unpacking to do? Didn't the moving van show up?"

"Yes, but I left it for later. I have to go to a party and I'm lost. I'm also late," she admitted.

The quiver in her lower lip was almost indiscernible but Chase noticed the slight movement. She wasn't so tough and suave as she tried to pretend. Being lost and late was causing her real distress.

"Where's the party?" Chase asked, although in the pit of his stomach he already knew the answer.

"The McDaniel Lodge on Lone Pine Lake."

"Well, you're almost there." He couldn't help himself; the edge of his lip curled upward in a smile.

She crossed her arms and frowned at him, the tilt of her head the only acknowledgment that he was right. "This isn't funny."

"I find it that way. Here I am, rescuing you a second time. Where would you be without me?"

"Sane?" she retorted, and Chase let out a roar of laughter.

"Ah, so I drive you crazy already. That's good to know. I'll file it away for future reference. So you're coming to my grandfather's party?"

"I am. Walter Peters invited me."

He stopped laughing then. "Walter? Don't tell me you're his… Is that how you got a job at McDaniel?"

Miranda glared at him as if he'd lost his mind. "That's a sick accusation. Absolutely not. Walter's my boss. We've known each other for years. He's like a father to me, that's all."

"Sorry. Just checking," Chase said, relieved.

Walter Peters and Chase's grandfather had been friends ever since Leroy had needed a supplier for McDaniel products, and he'd joined forces with Walter and the company he worked for. Each man served on the other's board of directors, and Leroy and Walter were constantly trading employees who needed promotions or different opportunities.

As for Miranda, Chase liked that she had fire. Most women didn't fight back. They were too eager to please. Miranda looked as if she'd like to tell him to go to hell. She probably would, if she had any idea how to get to the lodge.

She needed him. That was the only thing giving him the upper hand. For now, he'd take any advantage he could get. She raised his adrenaline more than the thirty miles he'd just clocked.

"Are you going to help me?" she demanded.

Chase nodded. "For a price."

"You're crazy. I can just drive back the way I came and ask directions in town."

"No, no." All of Chase's senses had heightened. The ride had made him a little heady, which must be the reason he wanted to press her against the car and ravage her mouth with his. The last mile would make for a good cooldown; his body needed one.

"I'm just saying I've come to your aid twice now. Don't you think you owe me a little reward for all my trouble?" he asked.

"Someone needs to teach you some manners."

Her lips held a little pucker, one he really liked.

"I'm teasing you, although I do plan to collect, so

be warned. If you want, follow me to the turnoff, then pass me and continue on until the road curves sharply to the left. You'll see a sign that the caterers put up, and you'll need to turn there. Just keep following the signs. You can't miss the tent or the parking."

"Okay." She seemed skeptical. "You can ride fast enough for me to follow you?"

"I'll sprint," he said. He put his sunglasses back on and locked his shoe into place. He grinned at her. "Be sure to keep up."

And with that, before she could even get into her car, he took off.

CHASE MCDANIEL HAD TO BE the most infuriating man she'd ever met, Miranda decided as she put her car in gear and took off after him. He hadn't even waited for her, just got on his bike and rode off at "sprint." His feet were flying.

She didn't know people could go that fast, except for maybe Lance Armstrong or one of those other racing guys. Chase could make that bike move, and she had to go a tad over the speed limit before she caught up with him. He slowed down then, and she followed at a safe distance.

Still, she got a great view of his backside. She had to admit his rear was nice. She'd seen him in a business suit and now in cycling shorts.

Naked, he was probably magnificent. He'd need a shower when he got back, and for a split second she had a vision of him standing under the spray, and her joining him….

She swallowed hard, and followed as he turned onto an asphalt road she had easily missed, since it was hardly wider than a driveway. She gave a quick wave and passed him, wanting to put distance between them.

From Chase's demeanor, she had to assume he didn't yet know anything about her or the scope of her new job. If he did, he probably would have ridden off and left her to find her own way.

She felt a bit guilty for not saying anything to him about her new position, but Leroy had insisted he wanted things handled his way. Miranda wasn't fond of subterfuge, but as this was her dream job, she'd agreed.

Now on the correct road, she easily found the signs, and soon drove up to the McDaniel estate. A parking attendant waved at her, and, when he found out she was staying at one of the guest cottages, showed her where to go. She climbed out and looked around, but Chase hadn't yet arrived.

"Ah! Miranda! There you are!" Walter boomed in greeting. She turned to find him standing on the screened porch of the cottage. "See you made it okay."

"I got lost a few times."

Walter's eyes twinkled. He was sixty-nine and retiring from his company presidency in two weeks. His departure was one of the reasons Miranda had accepted the McDaniel Manufacturing job. She might not get another opportunity to move up this fast ever again, and the company wouldn't be the same without Walter. There were also rumors of a forthcoming takeover by a competitor once Walter stepped down.

"Glad to see you made it in spite of me," he said, giving her a quick hug. "My directions aren't what they used to be. Heck, nothing's what it used to be. I'll be missing you come Tuesday."

"You've only got a week or two left yourself. Then

it's off on that round-the-world cruise with your wife. Speaking of which, where is she?"

"Our granddaughter Lucy had her baby Wednesday, so we're dividing and conquering. My wife loves Leroy, but not enough to put off holding her first great-grand-child."

"Good for her, and congrats," Miranda said. As she grabbed her suitcase from the trunk, she noticed Chase ride up. She watched him park the bike at the lodge and go inside without looking in her direction.

Bringing herself back to the moment, she carried her luggage inside. The cabin was small, with a living room–kitchen combination, shared bath and two bedrooms. Miranda didn't plan to stay long. She'd return to Chenille in the morning and spend Sunday afternoon and Memorial Day in her new apartment. She'd slept there last night, but the place hadn't yet felt like home. She had a lot of unpacking and other work to do before that happened. Not that any place had ever felt like home after her parents died.

"I'm going over to the lodge to visit with Leroy before the party starts. Do you want to come with me?" Walter asked from the porch.

Miranda glanced at herself in the bedroom mirror. She looked rumpled, and knew she had to face Chase again. He'd be showered and…

"I'll meet you at the party," she called to Walter, who yelled in agreement and shuffled off the porch. She tracked his movements from her window as he picked his way across the side yard. She'd been watching out for him for years. She was going to miss him. He called her his surrogate granddaughter, since none of his children had been interested in a business career.

While she loved working with Walter, the job at

McDaniel Manufacturing was her chance to get out from under his shadow and truly be her own person. She'd fought hard to reach this place in her life. For a second she blinked back tears, wishing her parents could see her now. She was so close to making all of her dreams come true.

And she wouldn't let anything ruin it.

Not even her attraction to Chase McDaniel.

Chapter Three

By six-thirty the party was in full swing. People milled everywhere, enjoying the warm weather, delicious appetizers and good company. Leroy held a place of honor, and since everyone wanted to speak with him, he was constantly surrounded.

Chase lifted the cup of beer to his lips, took a swallow and feigned interest in stories his lake neighbors were telling about their trip to Australia. But his concentration was shot. All he could think about was Miranda Craig.

She stood out of the sun on the opposite side of the tent. Walter Peters had taken her under his wing and was introducing her to everyone.

Chase lifted his beer and took another sip. The brew had grown warm, as he'd been holding the same cup for at least an hour. "That sounds great," he said at an appropriate juncture in the conversation, then added, "If you don't mind, I'm going to go check on how my grandfather is doing."

"Of course," Mrs. Schulz gushed. "We'll see more of you this summer, I'm sure."

"You will," he confirmed. The same crowd was

always at the country club restaurant on weekends, and he suspected he'd hear each of the Australia stories several times before the summer was out.

He wove his way through the crowd, stopping briefly to make certain his grandfather was okay. Chandy was sitting beside him. She nodded to Chase that everything was fine, and he moved on.

"Walter, I heard you were here," Chase said, reaching his target. "I'm sorry I missed you earlier."

"Chase!" The older man gave him a hug and a pat on the back. "Good to see you. Boy, you're rock solid. Must be all that exercise." Walter turned to Miranda. "Chase competes in triathlons."

"Only one or two a year, and only if I have time," he said smoothly, liking how her eyes widened. He stretched his hand forward. "Chase McDaniel."

"Miranda Craig," she said, the flicker in her eyes reflecting uncertainty.

"It's nice to meet you. I take it you worked for Walter," he said, as if they'd never met. He figured pretending they were strangers would allow her to salvage some pride. A woman as fierce as Miranda likely wouldn't want people to know she needed to be rescued. Twice.

"She did. Best employee I ever had. If I wasn't retiring I wouldn't let McDaniel steal her," Walter insisted proudly.

"Of course not," Chase agreed, with a smile that probably didn't quite hide the turmoil he felt. He liked Walter. He liked Miranda, as well, but in a totally different way. He brushed aside the uneasy feeling that something wasn't quite right. "Have you had a tour of Lone Pine?" he asked her.

"She arrived a little bit late and wanted to freshen

up," Walter confided, and Chase saw Miranda squirm. "So she missed the tour Chandy gave everyone earlier."

"She has to see the lodge," Chase said.

"Really, it's okay," Miranda protested.

"Oh no, it's a gem," Walter declared. "Finest place around. Christine and I love to come up here. We spend a week every August."

"I'd be happy to take her on a tour now," Chase offered.

"That's a great idea. Thanks, Chase. It would be a shame to come all this way and not see it," Walter told Miranda.

"Really, I—" she began.

"Hey, Walter!" The trio glanced over to see Leroy waving. "Come here a minute."

"Perfect timing," he said. "I'll catch up with you later. Go tour. Have fun. You'll love the place." Walter headed over to Leroy's circle.

"If I find out you arranged this, I'm likely to do you bodily harm," Miranda said quietly, so that only Chase could hear.

He chuckled. "I'd warn you against that. I might enjoy it too much. Come, let me show you around." He reached out and took her elbow. "Follow me."

"Seems like I'm doing that a lot," she murmured as they eased through the crowd and out from under the tent.

"Ah, but I get you where you need to be, don't I?" Chase's grin turned wicked. "Let me show you the lodge while it's empty. As Walter said, if you've come this far, you must see the place."

She hesitated, then nodded in agreement.

Chase led her across the yard, up the steps and inside.

"THIS IS BEAUTIFUL," Miranda breathed as they stepped into the great room. "I love it."

She'd seen pictures of fancy homes in upscale magazines. But they'd always looked cold and sterile. This was far less pretentious. It had a rustic, aged feel, like a timeless classic from a bygone era where life had been simpler.

The place was designed to be lived in. The hardwood floors showed wear from years of use. This was a family home, not an ostentatious attempt at showing off how much money the McDaniel family had. The room was friendly and inviting.

"So what do you think?" he asked.

She walked to the nine-foot-high, floor-to-ceiling windows at the front, and gazed out across the water. She'd grown up in an apartment building where large families were crammed into small units, and the next building was only a sidewalk width away. This room, with a ceiling that soared from nine to twenty-five feet high, was massive.

"It's lovely," she said.

He seemed pleased by her compliment. "Not too outdated?" he pressed.

She shook her head. "How can you even ask that? I think it's perfect." She gestured at the mission chairs placed strategically for the best lake view. "I could sit there for hours."

"I often do. When I was younger I remember my parents loving these chairs. I'd wake up, run downstairs and find them sitting here."

"It must be nice to have memories like that."

They stood near each other and watched a small sailboat cross the water. The lake wasn't deep enough to handle cabin cruisers and it wasn't long enough to attract huge Scarab-type boats. Because of that Lone Pine Lake catered to the pontoon boat and smaller runabout crowd, making it perfect for families. Below, a few of the older kids played on the paddleboats and a few kayaked. A canoe waited, overturned on the bank. The place screamed *home.*

"You're very lucky to have grown up here," she told him, trying to swallow past the lump in her throat.

Chase arched an eyebrow. "Even though there's no swimming pool in the backyard?"

She frowned. "Why would you need one when you have a lake?"

He shrugged. "An ex-girlfriend thought we should have a pool. Needless to say, she never visited. Seemed she wouldn't swim in anything that has fish poop."

Miranda made a disgusted face. "That's silly. I love going to the beach, and there are great ones as close as Lake Michigan."

"So you're not one of those girls afraid of getting your hair wet?"

She resisted the urge to tuck her short hair behind her ear, a nervous habit. "No. What good is the outdoors if you don't fully enjoy it? If you're dating people like that, no wonder you're all messed up."

"Me? Messed up?" He cupped her elbow, guided her down the hallway and gave her a peek at both the master suite and Leroy's office before showing her the other first-floor bedroom suite, where Chris, his wife and children stayed. "You didn't answer me. So I'm a disaster?"

"Yes. Of sorts." Better to be on the offensive. Anything to keep him from knowing the effect his light touch was having.

He led her back into the great room and then up the staircase to the second floor. "I'm injured."

She knew he was poking fun, and played along. "Don't be. Perhaps you should simply date better women."

"Such as you? You turned down my offer of lunch."

She ignored the bait. "Yes, because I'm not like the lingerie model wannabes I've seen you with."

His brows lifted. "I looked you up on Google," she admitted, "images and all. I wasn't too impressed. The media called you Iowa's heartthrob."

He covered his heart with the palm of his hand. "Ouch. You wound me further. That was years ago."

"Sure. You know, they call those kind of girls plastic for a reason. They look good, but that's about it."

"Maybe you're right." Chase leaned against the wall, and the hallway seemed to shrink. He was a big, sexy man. "That must be the reason I can't find true love. I'm dating the wrong kind of woman." His eyes dropped to her mouth.

"Could have something to do with it," she replied, her breath catching in her throat.

He edged nearer. "So what type of woman would fit me? You looked me up on Google. You saw all my past mistakes, my bad boy reputation. What do you think?"

He'd put her on the spot, but Miranda hadn't gotten this far without being able to think on her feet, despite her brain short-circuiting from his nearness. She stepped back. "If a woman's got any sense at all she'll know to steer clear of you."

"I'm really a great guy." He winked before continuing down the hallway.

He showed her his sisters' old bedrooms and then pushed the door to his open. Though the rooms on the first floor were larger, his wasn't shabby. It easily fit a queen-size bed, a dresser, a desk and a sitting area that overlooked the lake.

"Nice," Miranda said, hovering in the doorway while Chase went to look out the window.

He glanced over his shoulder and held out his hand. "I'm not going to throw you onto my bed and have my way with you. Come on. It's safe to step inside. This isn't a den of sin."

"I know that," she snapped, feeling slightly foolish. What was the big deal? It was just a bedroom. His stuff was in the drawers. A wet towel hung in the bathroom. A dirty pair of white socks lay on the floor by some running shoes. A pair of plaid pajama bottoms peeked out from under the rumpled red comforter.

As much as she might want to step into the room, it was just too personal. Chase's magnetism overwhelmed her. He made a tsking noise, as if disappointed she wouldn't take a risk.

Chemistry was a— She cut off the mental expletive. Men like Chase should be outlawed. Their mere presence was lethal.

"You're missing a great view of the lake," he cajoled.

"I know." She shook her head and opted for safety, and a few minutes later they were back downstairs.

Chase opened the front door, led her down some steps and out onto the front lawn. "We'll tour the boathouse and then head back to the party."

"Okay," she said, following him along a narrow stone path down a gently sloping hill. The boathouse wasn't actually over the water. Instead, the cedar frame building sat back about ten feet from the edge of the lake. They entered through the side door. "Wow," she breathed.

She'd expected a square room filled with life preservers and oars. The room contained those, but everything was neatly organized in cubbies. Rather than being the storage shed she'd expected, the boathouse functioned almost like a den. There was a bar and stools. A few tables. A dartboard, a foosball game, a billiard table and a small television set.

"This is where we used to hang out all the time." Chase made a sweeping gesture. "This was teen central."

"I noticed there didn't seem to be any video games or TVs up in the lodge."

"Never have been. The lodge is a place to get away from the world. The boathouse is a place to play and have fun. Imagine four kids plus all their friends. It got wild. We would move up here with our grandma the moment school let out, and friends would come and go all summer."

"What about Leroy?"

"My grandfather has a three-day workweek from Memorial Day to Labor Day. He's done it for years."

"Must be nice."

Chase grinned. "It pays to be the boss. As for us kids, we sometimes got bored. But usually we kept busy. No couch potatoes in my family. My grandfather installed that ballerina bar and those mirrors for Cecilia."

Miranda glanced over, seeing her and Chase's reflection. She swallowed. He looked so assured and comfortable. This was his home.

"So what made you choose to relocate to Podunkville?" he asked.

"I wouldn't call Chenille that," she protested. "Small towns are charming. I've found the people lots more easygoing than those in Chicago. And even friendlier to strangers."

"That's only so they can gossip about you at Maxine's, the most popular restaurant downtown." He grinned and then became serious. "So what exactly are you doing for us? Why'd you leave Walter's company? Were you as high up as you could go? That's usually why we get people from Walter."

"It was a rather last minute decision. I had planned on staying where I was after Walter retired, but there are takeover rumors and the board is unsettled. Signs were that a move might be best."

"I'll warn you, the shopping's not very good in Chenille. We're forty miles from the nearest mall."

"Malls are overrated."

He chuckled. "I thought all girls loved to shop. My sisters are deadly."

Maybe those who had money saw retail therapy as a sport, but shopping for Miranda had always meant being frugal. Her purse strings had loosened these past few years, but she couldn't break the habit of budgeting. She had a few school loans to pay off before indulging in anything frivolous. And she had to save for retirement. "I'm not 'all girls,'" she finally told him.

"I've already figured that part out."

While she'd been lost in thought he'd moved dangerously close. Worse, she was backed up against a bar stool. She had no way to escape and she wasn't sure she would if she could. Every nerve ending in her body tingled with awareness. "What are you doing?" she breathed.

"Cashing in on what you owe me."

"Really?" she asked, trying to regain control. "When did I get in your debt?"

He thought for a second. "That came out wrong. I'm claiming my reward for rescuing you."

"I don't remember promising you anything," she said, but his head lowered. She froze. He was going to kiss her.

She should tell him no. Fight it. Get away from Chase McDaniel and back to the party as quickly as her legs could carry her. That would be the rational thing to do.

But she couldn't. He was like rocky road ice cream. Impossible to resist. His lips lightly touched hers and didn't disappoint. He kissed her gently, as if testing how far she'd let him go.

Her body quickened. She wanted him to deepen the kiss, and as if reading her mind, he began to really kiss her. She let herself taste him, let him slide his tongue inside to connect with hers.

He was divine. Sure, she'd been kissed before, but something about kissing Chase felt different. It felt perfect. But it was also terribly wrong.

She pulled back, trying to ignore the flood of sensations rushing through her. What he'd roused with one kiss had warning signs flashing in her head. "I think you've had enough of a reward," she said. Her voice came out huskier than she would have liked.

His gaze locked on to hers and his lips parted. For a moment she thought he'd try to change her mind. Then he stepped away and let her go. "Shall we head back to the party then?"

The abrupt way he dismissed what had happened made her knees wobble. She couldn't believe she'd forgotten her reserve and fallen under the spell of his playboy charms. He seemed to live for adventure. And she'd been just another challenge. Now that he'd succeeded, game over. Time to move on to the next conquest.

She followed him from the boathouse and toward the tent. Dinner had been served and people were sitting at tables eating and laughing.

"Shall we eat?" Chase asked.

"Sure," Miranda agreed.

Places had been saved for them at the head table, and after going through the buffet line, they settled in their seats. Miranda tried to eat, but the fact that she'd kissed Chase McDaniel smarted. She wasn't easy, yet she'd succumbed like a dog rolling over for a pat on its stomach. Disappointment at her behavior made her lose her appetite, so she picked at her food, while Leroy and Walter shared stories of becoming friends and building companies.

"Mine was always a family business. Even now we control the stock," Leroy boasted.

"Yeah, but I proved to my boss you didn't have to be family to get ahead. I'm a self-made man."

"And I'm not?" Leroy countered. They loved to one-up each other, a friendly game they'd played for years.

"I've survived two mergers," Walter claimed.

"Speaking of which, what's with this latest take-over?" his old friend asked.

"Is something wrong with your food?" Chase leaned close and gestured to Miranda's plate as Walter began to describe the situation in detail.

"It's delicious," she replied. The food *was* superb, and she forced herself to eat a bite.

The gall of the man, anyway. Why had he kissed her? Sure, it was only a kiss, but for some reason she couldn't let it go the way Chase obviously had. He'd probably kissed plenty of women like that, which showed her inexperience. She also felt guilty. She'd enjoyed his touch too much. It had been awhile since she'd dated. Heck, she hadn't had a real relationship in over a year, and Manuel had only been using her to close a sales deal and get a promotion at his company.

The night slipped on, and Chase asked her to dance. Despite her resolve to keep distance between them, she went. She wanted to be in his arms, to see if her earlier reaction was a fluke. She also wanted to speak with him.

"I need to tell you something," she said as the slow number ended. She had to talk to him about her job. Given what had happened between them, it was the right thing to do. Otherwise, working together would be awkward. It probably would be anyway. He was like chocolate cake. She loved eating it, but afterward felt guilty for indulging.

"What is it?" Chase asked.

She opened her mouth.

"Chase!"

Miranda closed her lips and tried not to grimace as an older couple came forward.

"You look fantastic," the woman gushed. "I haven't seen you in, what, ten years?"

"This is Leroy's second cousin Laura and her husband, Cliff." Chase made the introductions. "They live in Paris."

"Yes, but we wouldn't have missed Leroy's eightieth for the world."

Miranda, seeing the conversation would be ongoing, soon slipped away.

"Having fun?" Walter asked as she returned to her seat.

"Loads," she said, her gaze seeking out Chase. She knew he'd hate her once his grandfather took the stage.

Not five minutes later that moment arrived, sealing Miranda's fate. Her window of opportunity to tell Chase the truth and set things right had closed.

Leroy grasped the microphone in one hand and asked for everyone's attention. Chase finished chatting with his relatives and moved to the side of the room, joining his siblings. Miranda slipped into the chair next to Walter.

"I saw you and Chase dance. I'm glad you'll be able to work well together," Walter told her.

"Yeah." Miranda didn't want to tell him that was doubtful after tonight. She listened as Leroy thanked everyone for coming, before acknowledging and introducing his family.

Then he said, "As you know, I'm eighty." He paused and waited out a few hoots and hollers. "But contrary to the rumors, I'm not retiring. I've decided to stay until this time next year. Still, I want to start easing my way out slowly."

Leroy looked over the crowd, which consisted of business colleagues, friends, neighbors and family. "To achieve my objective and to make the transition smoother, I've decided to restructure the top of McDaniel Manufacturing. My good friend Walter Peters and I discussed ideal candidates for the new position I'm creating. It'll be third in line, behind me and behind Chase, my grandson."

Everyone glanced at Chase and he gave a short nod. His face remained taut and impassive, even though Leroy smiled at him.

"In fact, it's been so hush-hush that this is the first time I've brought it up, even to Chase. However, since I *am* the CEO…" The few board members present laughed. They would rubber-stamp anything Leroy wanted.

"I'm calling this new spot a vice presidency, and the person I've hired to fill the position is here with us tonight."

Walter touched Miranda's arm in a show of support. She needed it. Even though she wasn't looking at Chase, she could sense him watching her, and her skin heated.

"I'd like to introduce Miranda Craig as the new second vice president of McDaniel Manufacturing," Leroy continued, and somehow she stood and briefly waved to the crowd.

Only after she sat down did she dare glance at Chase. His grandfather continued to talk, but the speech faded into a background hum as Chase and Miranda's eyes connected.

With effort, she managed not to avert her head. She hated what she read on his face. His initial shock had turned into anger and the tight expression guaranteed payback. Since Leroy hadn't told Chase anything about Miranda, he clearly thought she'd been coy and flirtatious. He thought she'd played him.

In a sense, maybe she had. She knew what many others in the room did not. Chase was going on forced sabbatical. She was the one who was going to take over his job. She was his grandfather's choice for the next CEO should Chase fail to return.

As she watched, Chase lifted his glass to her in a mock salute. A feeling of foreboding settled over her. He wasn't offering her good wishes. Miranda wasn't that naive. Gone was the passion, replaced with something much deadlier. Chase wasn't conceding an inch.

This was war.

Chapter Four

Chase had never thought of himself as the type of person who would be able to commit murder. But as he stared at Miranda, he wanted nothing more than to wring her pretty little neck until she begged for mercy or at least apologized.

He'd kissed her! He'd flirted with the enemy.

He took a deep breath, calming himself as Cecilia approached. "You okay?"

"Of course," Chase replied through gritted teeth. How could he not have seen this? Easy. McDaniel had thousands of employees and there were always jobs open. Never in a million years would Chase have expected his grandfather to create a second vice president position or to bring in an outsider to fill that niche.

His sister touched his cheek, and Chase unclenched his jaw and forced a fake smile to his face.

"That's better," she said. She knew him far too well. "Gotta keep up appearances."

"Yeah." Chase gave a nod of acknowledgment to a passerby. He lifted his glass and saluted another.

After his one beer, he'd been drinking water most of the evening. He hadn't wanted anything dulling his senses.

"Here they come," Cecilia whispered, as Leroy led Miranda through the crowd.

Chase clenched his fists and tried to keep his smile from slipping.

"Chase," Leroy said in greeting a few moments later. "I know you met Miranda earlier. There isn't anyone more competent or more suited to this position than her. She'll start Tuesday. I expect you to show her the ropes."

Chase would like to show her a noose. Sure, most people would love to be in his position. As soon as Miranda took over, he'd be free to enjoy a life of leisure. He could collect his salary and, for one year, do whatever he wanted. How awesome was that? Trouble was, he already had six weeks vacation time annually, and hardly ever took any. He loved McDaniel and he loved his job. The last thing he wanted was some upstart replacement coming in and messing with his company—no matter how gorgeous she was.

"I'm sure Miranda and I will get along just fine," he said evenly, hoping Leroy wouldn't notice the frost in his voice.

"I hope that's the case," his grandfather said.

"I'm Cecilia," his sister said suddenly, inserting herself into the conversation as a diversion.

"Miranda." The two women shook hands. "So you're a ballerina."

"That's right." Cecilia steered her a few feet away, to diffuse the tension.

"You could have told me," Chase murmured, the moment he and Leroy were as alone as two people at a party could be.

His grandfather stiffened. "What? That the person replacing you was a woman? I didn't think you were a chauvinist."

"I'm not. I'm upset that you blindsided me with all of this. The sabbatical. A second vice president. Her. And trust me, I know she's a woman!"

Leroy's eyes narrowed. "Don't tell me you already hit on her."

"I am not a Casanova!" Chase protested, but not fast enough.

The older man's jaw dropped. "Chase. Please tell me you didn't."

"Well, how was I supposed to know who she was? We met Friday morning outside McDaniel. That's why I was late arriving yesterday afternoon. I changed her flat tire. I asked her to lunch. I flirted with her again in the boathouse. Now I look and feel like an idiot." *And I kissed her.*

"I'm sorry. I did what I thought was best. I didn't want you more stressed than you already are."

Chase reined in his temper. He and Leroy were a lot alike, and he loved his grandfather dearly. He'd made sure they wanted for nothing growing up.

"It will be fine. All I have to do is train her and then go, right? That's your plan?"

"Yes, but—" Leroy began.

Chase straightened. "I am a professional. I will treat her with the utmost respect. I won't do anything to jeopardize the company or its reputation."

"That's not what I meant." His grandfather paused. "None of this has ever been about you being incompetent. It's never been meant as a slap in the face. I just want to give you the opportunity I never had. What you never had. A choice."

Chase knew that. Still, his pride had been injured, and he'd overreacted. He'd also just kissed the woman taking his job. He reached out and gave his grandfather a quick hug. "I understand. I may not like it, but I understand."

"Trust me, you'll be grateful for this year. You just don't see it now."

Chase sighed as he let the anger and the blow to his pride go, at least where his grandfather was concerned. As for Miranda, the jury was still out.

THE PARTY HAD WOUND DOWN a bit before midnight, give or take a few stragglers not quite ready to call it an evening. Leroy and Walter had left around eleven-thirty. They were both notorious early risers, and had stayed up way later than their norm. Miranda had lingered about twenty minutes longer, but Chase hadn't approached her. She'd thought about talking to him, and had even headed in his direction, but it was as if he'd sensed her coming. He'd disappeared before she made it through the crowd.

She sighed and rolled over in bed now, staring up at the ceiling.

Even though the mattress was comfortable, she was too keyed up to sleep. She'd been tossing and turning for what felt like hours. She pressed the button on her cell phone, brightening the display. It was a little after one.

She swung her feet to the floor and stood up. The best thing to do in a situation like this was to clear her head. Miranda pulled on yoga pants, traded her nightshirt for a T-shirt and slipped on flip-flops. Then she left the cottage.

She'd lived in the city her whole life, and the stillness of the night seemed foreign yet comforting. Low voltage solar lights provided just enough of a glow that she could see the path, and the moon cast a swath of light over the grassy slope leading down to the lake.

The water itself shimmered, parts of it reflective, while other areas remained dark and mysterious. She looked heavenward, gasping at the number of stars visible. She'd never seen a night sky quite as sharp and clear.

In Chicago the city lights muted the universe's brilliance. Her aunt hadn't been rich, so Miranda and her sister had lived far from any Lake Michigan view. Open space hadn't been grassy meadows, but empty lots filled with rubble and weeds.

She inhaled deeply now, filling her lungs with fresh northern air untainted by car exhaust.

So this was how the other half lived. Miranda had seen those television shows that featured celebrity houses. She hadn't necessarily wanted something like that, but she'd longed for more than her aunt's small apartment on the wrong side of the interstate.

She planned to exceed every one of her parents' expectations, to make a better life for herself and her sister.

Miranda made her way toward the dock. She reached the end, took off her shoes and sat down. Her dangling feet didn't quite reach the water, but its gentle lapping created a breeze that tickled her toes.

She sighed happily. Here she was, in this wonderful place, ready to embark on something new.

"Guilt keeping you awake?"

Chase's familiar voice made her jolt, and even though she was seated, she tumbled off balance before righting herself.

He stood only a few feet behind her, which meant he must have crept up.

"Why would I feel guilty, and how long have you been standing there?" she shot back. He stepped forward and settled next to her. He was still dressed in what he'd worn to the party, putting her at a slight disadvantage in her thin T-shirt with nothing underneath.

"Saw you come down and figured I'd find out why."

"Don't worry. I'm not trying to steal anything else that's precious to you."

"Testy, I see. Maybe you are guilty."

She sighed. Somehow Chase always had the upper hand, even when the chips were down.

"I just needed a few moments alone," Miranda replied. "I probably should go. I have to drive home tomorrow."

"Have you ever been out on the water?" he asked, removing his shoes as if he hadn't heard a word she'd said.

She shook her head. "I've never been on any boat, except for Walter's anniversary cruise on Lake Michigan."

"Then you were a deprived child."

Perhaps it was the way he said it that made her bristle and forget her urge to leave. "Not all of us were as fortunate as you. Not all of us grew up with a silver spoon in our mouths and a job waiting for us."

"Yeah, a job that you're determined to take away."

"I'm only a vice president, and a second one at that. Behind you," Miranda reminded him, ignoring the fact that she'd danced giddily around her studio apartment the day she'd officially gotten the job.

Chase didn't buy her explanation. "Semantics. You know as well as I do that my grandfather doesn't intend for me to come back. And don't pretend that it's not in your plan to make yourself so damn indispensable that even if I do return, the board will back you and not me for his job."

"That's not my intention," she protested, despite

having fantasized about doing just that. What woman didn't let herself dream, when the possibilities seemed limitless? At least they had on the day Leroy hired her.

Chase scoffed. "Yeah, I believe that as much as I believe you just forgot to tell me about your job. We may have encountered each other by accident, but your actions once we met were calculated and deliberate."

"Really, they weren't," Miranda said. She had to work with Chase. They needed to get off on the right foot if he was going to be responsible for her training. "Perhaps we should start over," she suggested. "Give ourselves until Tuesday to calm down and put this behind us."

"And you really believe in that drivel? That we can pretend nothing happened?"

"People do it all the time." She jutted out her chin. "I want this job. This is a dream opportunity for me. You leave permanently or come back after a year, I don't care. My aunt never thought I'd get this far. I made something of my life and that's all that matters."

He stared at her a little more intently now, as if trying to figure out what she wasn't telling him. But she refused to elaborate. "So whatever grudge you have, I'm here to do a job. Nothing more," she finished.

"I wish I could believe that."

She squared her shoulders. "It doesn't matter what you believe. It's the truth."

"Truth is relative. Often meaningless. I kissed you today. That's the truth. But I guess it *was* meaningless. Just…"

"An awkward mistake," she interjected quickly. Thinking about Chase's mouth on hers had her temperature skyrocketing.

"Another mistake to be forgotten on Tuesday, as well, I gather."

He sounded disappointed, which was funny considering he'd reacted so coldly in the boathouse.

"So we start over, as if we'd never met?" he asked.

"Fresh start on Tuesday," she agreed, aware that the air above the dock had become charged.

"So *today* is meaningless," he said. "I forgive you and you forgive me."

Aware that somehow she'd started down a slippery slope, but not sure where it was leading her, she nodded. "Exactly."

"Seems I need something for which to be forgiven," Chase replied.

"This is the best way to proceed for both of us…" Miranda suddenly realized he wasn't listening. Instead, all of his attention was focused on her mouth. He reached forward and tugged her to him.

The man can kiss was the last recognizable thought Miranda managed before she started whimpering in response to the delightful plunder of her lips. Then she was kissing him once again, overcome with the desperate need to get as close to him as possible.

One of his hands slid up to her neck, the other moved to cup her breast, covered only by the thin T-shirt fabric. Her breath caught and her body twitched as his fingers found pleasure points and sent heat pooled between her legs. Then coolness suddenly descended as Chase pulled away and got to his feet.

Miranda covered her breasts with her arms, realizing she could have easily made love to him right here on the dock, out in the open under the stars.

"See you Tuesday," he said, the slight rasp in his voice the only hint that she'd had any physical effect on him at all. He then strode off the dock and up the hill, leaving his shoes behind.

She stared at the loafers, resisting the urge to toss them in the lake and watch them sink to the murky bottom. He'd switched passion on and off once again, the jerk! Worse, she'd let him.

She trembled as she stood, determined to get off the dock before he reached his room and could see her from the window.

Grabbing her own shoes, she fled barefoot toward the cabin.

CHASE STOOD IN THE shadows by the lodge and watched her escape. He needed to go back for his shoes. He also planned to jump into the cold lake. Kissing her had made him hard as a rock. He'd wanted nothing more than to lay her back and sink himself deep inside her.

He grimaced. Miranda Craig's idea of forgiving and forgetting was ridiculous.

Hearing her cabin door click shut, he walked down to the lake. Never had he been this affected by a woman. Sure, he loved having sex. But kissing Miranda had felt different, and not because she was forbidden fruit, or he had some Neanderthal idea of proving to her who was boss.

Maybe it was his need for dominance that had led to the kiss, but once his lips had touched hers he'd forgotten all about control. He'd forgotten his anger and suspicion. He'd forgotten, once again, that she was the enemy.

He'd never experienced such overwhelming, mindless passion before. Too bad the circumstances around her arrival in his life were so terribly wrong.

He reached the dock, stripped down to his boxers and dived in, letting the cold water soothe his soul.

Unfortunately, he knew that instead of finding closure by kissing Miranda, he'd simply opened a whole new can of worms.

Chapter Five

As if responding to the weekend's upheaval, on Tuesday morning the heavens opened and the skies above Chenille poured sheets of hard, pelting rain.

Miranda gathered her umbrella closer, but the strong wind whipped underneath and blew it inside out, the thin metal frame no match for nature's wrath.

She fought to tug the umbrella back into its correct shape. Despite her raincoat, by the time she'd reached the main doors of McDaniel Manufacturing, she was drenched.

A quick glance in the mirror of the lobby bathroom showed that her short black hair had frizzed. Her carefully applied makeup had washed away, and her mascara had proved exactly why it was so reasonably priced.

She quickly combed her hair. Nothing she could do about that—it would stay wet. She made a few quick repairs to her makeup, refusing to be late on the first day of work. Her instructions were to meet Chase in approximately…

Miranda quickened her pace. She had three minutes to reach the executive floor. She dug into her purse, removed the key card she'd received Friday and swiped her way through security and into the elevator that would take her to the seventh and highest floor. She'd toured the premises already, and her feet flew as she reached her office, where, leaning against the door frame, Chase waited. He glanced at his watch.

Inwardly she cursed. She'd wanted a few moments to compose herself before she went to meet him.

Instead, here he was, lounging in her doorway, looking better than any man had a right to. Gorgeous and sexy as hell. The dark blue suit showed off his broad shoulders and the red power tie drew attention to a chest with muscles too well defined to be completely hidden beneath his shirt.

She snapped her gaze upward, but not before his lips curled into an infuriating grin. He knew she'd been looking, and that she liked what she saw.

Her only hope was that she affected him, too. But he didn't appear to be aroused so much as amused. Obviously, whatever passion they'd shared was in the past. She'd said "start over" and Chase was clearly ready to do just that.

"Thought I'd take the stress off and meet you here," he said easily, as if he didn't have a care in the world. "So are you ready?" he asked, his brisk tone all business.

She blinked. She couldn't let physical attraction distract her. She'd been in control of her life for far too long to let something as silly as a knee-jarring kiss throw her off track.

"Let me just put this on my desk," she replied, hefting her leather briefcase, an expensive gift to herself upon landing the job. It had been her one indulgence.

Miranda placed her deformed umbrella in a corner

and hung her raincoat on the peg behind the door. She grabbed a pad of notepaper and a pen from her desk. "I'm ready."

"Can I get you something to drink? Tea? Coffee?" he asked, leading the way down the hallway to his office. He rounded a corner, stopping by his secretary's desk. "Ms. Craig would like some…" He paused and waited expectantly, putting her on the spot.

"Some water would be nice. I'm Miranda Craig."

"It's nice to meet you. I'm Carla," Chase's executive assistant replied as she got to her feet. "Your usual?" she asked Chase.

"Perfect." He nodded at Carla and motioned Miranda into his office.

"You know, I really could have gotten my own water," she told him once they were out of earshot and seated at a small six-seater conference table.

"It's fine," he replied crisply, and she had the impression she'd made a misstep. Less than a minute later Carla entered with the beverages. She also carried two spiral-bound portfolios under her right arm, and she placed them in front of Chase. He waited until she left before sliding one of the binders toward Miranda. Miranda steeled herself. She would prove her hiring was no mistake.

He opened the front cover and she did the same. "Let's get started."

By LUNCHTIME, Chase had to admit one thing: Miranda was quick on her feet and a sharp learner. During the course of the morning he'd gone over everything from his job description to the inner workings of the corporation. He'd presented flow charts and spreadsheets of the company's holdings and financials. He'd shown her the newly approved five-year plan for future growth.

He hadn't cut her any slack. As his replacement, she had a lot to learn in a very short time. He'd been as hard on her as he would have been on anyone else, maybe harder, all the while secretly hoping she'd fall on her face. Some part of him, obviously not his usual chivalrous side, had hoped that she might not grasp everything, which would give Chase an excuse to fight his grandfather's decision.

Now, after seeing how bright and capable she was, he had to admit he'd been wrong. She'd already done a number on his equilibrium. Finding her his business equal was the icing on the cake. Unfortunately, he couldn't indulge.

"Lunch," he told her.

She smiled at him, and he fought to keep his focus on business. He liked her green eyes. He liked her lips. He liked everything about her, which made leaving his company, and her, torturous. "You do eat lunch, right?"

"Yes," Miranda said.

He arched a brow, wondering why she hadn't moved yet. "Shall we meet back here in an hour?" he asked.

"Uh, sure." She rose to her feet slowly. Her forehead creased as she gathered up her purse. "So we don't have lunch plans?"

"No. Were we supposed to?"

She shook her head, a little too quickly, Chase realized, wincing. Since it was her first day, his grandfather had probably told her Chase would take her to lunch. Another thing Leroy had conveniently forgotten to mention. Chase hoped there weren't any more surprises.

He stood. "I'll take you to Maxine's."

Now she looked panicked. "It's not necessary. I haven't seen my office for longer than ten minutes. I have a box of stuff in my trunk that I need to bring in and unload...."

"You can do that tomorrow," Chase said. His chivalry had returned, and now that he'd made his decision, he could be as stubborn as Leroy. "You have to experience Maxine's."

"Seriously, I don't need a pity offer."

He held up a hand to stop her. "I don't do anything out of pity. I'll meet you by the elevator in five minutes. Don't be late."

Then, before she could protest further, Chase left the room.

CHASE'S OFFICE SEEMED a lot bigger now that he'd exited. Miranda studied the space, hoping to learn something about the man whose job she would take over for a year.

Framed artwork, diplomas and pictures decorated the walls. In one corner, near a bookcase, a saddle rested on a custom stand. She stood and went over, noticing a few ribbons and trophies. There was also a framed photo of a young man on a horse, roping a steer. She lifted it to take a closer look. Chase, she realized.

She set the picture down, noticing a recent photo of his family on a shelf nearby. Next to that was an older family portrait, of four kids and two adults. She swallowed as she realized the latter were Chase's parents. The whole family was frozen in time, all happy and untouched by the tragedy soon to befall them.

She had a picture like that herself.

"You're still here," Carla said, entering the office. "I'm going to straighten up. Chase told me he's taking you to Maxine's. Fantastic food. You'll love it."

"I hope so," Miranda replied. Perhaps she'd misunderstood Leroy saying that Chase would take her to lunch.

Since she'd lingered in his office, she didn't have time to freshen up, so she headed straight for the elevator. It didn't surprise her that he was already waiting. As soon as he saw her, he pressed the Down button.

She'd eaten lunch with Walter and other company executives dozens of times, but Chase's waiting for her felt almost like a date. It wasn't, though, so she'd better get herself together, and fast.

"Thank you for changing your plans. I appreciate the gesture. I'm sorry it was sprung on you."

"It's nothing." Chase entered the elevator behind her and pressed the button for the lobby. "I should have been more sensitive about welcoming you to the company properly. With anyone else I probably would have. It *is* your first day, and of course I should be taking you to lunch. I've been a bit of a cad."

Miranda didn't have any illusions that she and Chase would kiss, make up and be friends, but she recognized the masked apology. She acknowledged it with a slight nod of her head before changing the subject. "I noticed the saddle in your office. Do you still ride?"

"Not like that. I stopped roping about ten years ago. Couldn't quite get rid of saddle, though. For years it was a part of me."

"You shouldn't. It's a memory. A good one, right? You enjoyed it."

He shrugged. "I did okay. I earned a few ribbons and belt buckles."

The elevator door opened and they stepped out and crossed the lobby to the main entrance. The rain had let up, but puddles remained. The sun was starting to break through the clouds, which was a good thing, since Miranda had left her umbrella in her office.

"I'm parked over here." Chase led her toward a compact SUV with a bike rack on the back. "When I leave, this will be your spot."

Which would be good for rainy days, as it was closer to the entrance, Miranda noted.

Chase opened the front passenger door and she climbed in. The drive took under five minutes, since Maxine's was in a storefront on Main Street. Chenille's downtown was pristine and unspoiled by time, the buildings old-fashioned and charming.

"I like all the little shops down here. I haven't had a chance to explore them yet."

"They'll have most everything you need, especially if you don't want to drive. The nearest Wal-Mart is twenty miles west. We aren't a big enough town to support our own, which is fine by me."

"I found it. I went there yesterday to pick up some things."

Chase held open the outer door. "Maxine's has been here for about twenty years, but the building is much older. It's on the historic registry. When you get inside take a look at the millwork. It's all original."

He opened the second door and they stepped inside.

"Chase," the hostess called. "How are you today?"

"Fantastic. Diane, this is Miranda Craig. She's McDaniel's new vice president. This is her first day and her first time eating here."

"Nice to meet you, and welcome to Chenille. I hope you enjoy your meal and that you like it enough to come back often. Your usual table okay today, Chase?"

"That'll be fine," he replied as she grabbed two menus. He put his hand lightly on Miranda's back to guide her. Despite the layers of clothing, her body immediately reacted to his touch, and she bit her lip.

As she followed the hostess, Chase's hand suddenly fell away. Miranda glanced behind and noticed he'd stopped for a second to greet someone. But he was there to pull out her chair before Diane had time to set the menus down.

"Sorry for that," he said.

"I guess you know just about everyone in town." Miranda glanced around the restaurant. Chase hadn't been kidding about the woodwork. The place reminded her of an old tavern, complete with heavy wooden tables. Maxine's had several rooms, and just about every seat was full.

"You'll quickly get to know the movers and shakers of Chenille. Most of them eat lunch here every day. If they're still there I'll introduce you on the way out. That's Martin Villas. He's president of one of the local banks, and he's with Butch Ifland, the former mayor. Butch is running for county commissioner."

"Your town seems pretty tight-knit."

"There are only three hundred kids in the high school. My graduating class had seventy-three students."

Miranda put the burgundy-colored cloth napkin in her lap. "There were over two thousand in my high school. No one really knew anyone. I was happy to get out. I didn't have many friends, since I didn't get there until the middle of my junior year."

"You transferred midyear?"

She fingered her napkin. "It wasn't my choice. My parents died."

"I'm sorry. That must have been hard." Chase took a sip of his water and Miranda appreciated the empathy in his voice. At least he hadn't pitied her. She'd had enough of that over the years.

She picked up the menu, but had no idea what to order. She set it down again and realized he was waiting for her to continue. "The only family my sister and I had left was my aunt. She wasn't too thrilled about taking us in. That's one of the reasons this job is so important to me."

"Then I guess we have two things in common," Chase said.

He meant both the job and their parents' deaths. She hadn't really thought about having anything in common with Chase. Maybe this was something on which they could build a working relationship.

The waitress arrived to take their orders. Although Chase chose the special, a Reuben sandwich, Miranda played it safe and decided on a sliced turkey sandwich and a side garden salad. She reached for her water as Chase spoke again.

"Do you mind if I ask you what happened?"

Miranda stared at him, then tried to lighten the moment. "Who are you and what have you done with the Chase who grilled me all morning?"

"Truce. It's lunchtime." When he grinned, she realized that somewhere along the line his smile had grown on her. He wasn't a bad guy; he was just in a bad situation.

"The answer is that a drunk driver hit my parents. My father died instantly. My mother survived the accident, but didn't have the will to live without my dad. She died six months later. I was sixteen."

"That must have been hard."

Miranda sighed. "I've managed."

"But it's affected you. It's tough. I know. It doesn't make you weak to admit it."

"You're right. It's made me strong. It's the reason I'm so driven. My younger sister and I are nine years apart in age. She's the reason I stayed in Chicago. My aunt and I didn't get along, but I refused to leave Linda behind. She was only seven when the accident happened."

"So you took care of her."

Miranda shrugged. "As best I could. When I could finally afford to move out I took her with me. My job allowed me to send her to college. My parents wanted degrees for both of us. She's going to be a psychologist, so she needs a Ph.D. She's finishing this year. Even with tons of financial aid, you'd be amazed at all the costs entailed. It's been a struggle throughout. During college I always had part-time jobs, and worked as many hours as I could."

"My grandparents stepped in for my siblings and me," Chase murmured. "We never had to worry about finances like you did. I've been a jerk in prejudging you. I'm sorry. I doubt I could have done what you did."

"My past is past." She reached for her drink, holding the iced tea like a barrier. Chase as Mr. Sensitivity was disconcerting. He couldn't start being nice now! Although that was what part of her wanted, warning bells in her head forecasted danger. If he could be like this all the time, no wonder women fell for him.

He pressed on. "I have to disagree that you get to leave the past behind. Sometimes I wish I could, but it becomes a part of you. It's always in the back of your mind, that little 'what if.' What would my life be like had that day never happened?"

"Yeah," she replied. He did understand. "You try not to think about it."

"But you have to. *I* do. Every day. That's why my grandfather concocted this plan. You do understand that

I don't want to leave for a year. Not only did he force me, but he sprang the news on me."

"I know. When Leroy hired me he told me you weren't going to be happy. He said you'd be pretty resistant. I wanted to tell you who I was when we met, but he said he wanted things handled his way, and who was I to disagree?"

Chase frowned. "I guess hearing your explanation helps me understand why you kept the truth to yourself."

The hairs on Miranda's neck rose. "I never meant to mislead you."

"Doesn't matter. Even though I hate the idea, it's what he wants for me. I can't deny him something he feels so strongly about."

"Of course you care about his wishes. You love him." Impulsively she reached out and covered Chase's hand with hers. His skin was warm beneath her palm. His gaze locked on to hers and her breath lodged in her chest. Or maybe her heart had missed a beat.

Whatever had just happened, she felt a sudden kinship with Chase. She also felt the chemistry between them simmering just below the surface and threatening to bubble forth.

The waitress approached with their food, and Miranda snatched her hand back. She glanced around the room, but no one appeared to be paying attention. However, she was extremely aware that she'd been touching Chase, in Maxine's, where, he'd told her, everyone spread Chenille's latest gossip.

Pretending to be engrossed with her sandwich, she removed the top slice of bread and added some honey mustard.

Chase watched her thoughtfully. "Just so you know, that's not going to work."

She looked at him. "What? I happen to like honey mustard on sandwiches."

The corner of his mouth inched upward. "Always quick on your feet, aren't you? But you know what I mean. You showed empathy in a public place. You touched me and people noticed. And yes, they're going to gossip. But stop worrying. You didn't do anything wrong. I liked you touching me."

He didn't understand, she realized. "They'll think we're dating. They don't know who I am."

He shifted forward. "So? They'll find out otherwise and that will be that. No big deal."

"Yeah, but what if they think I dated you to get the position?" She frowned as she thought of something else. "How many different women do you bring here, anyway?"

"None, so relax. This is where I bring business colleagues." Chase reached for a French fry.

Maybe she *was* overreacting. He knew the town better than she did. "Still…"

His shoulders tightened and he leaned back in his chair, crossing his arms over his chest. "Don't worry. I got your point. You've mentioned my reputation enough. Heck, maybe that's what I should do for my vacation. Go to Hollywood and pick up a blond playmate. Although she'd probably be a bit too 'plastic.' And I doubt she'd want to return with me to Podunkville when my exile is over."

"Forget my early commiseration. I think you're being ungrateful," Miranda told him before she could bite back the words. She didn't like the change in Chase. Mr. Sensitivity had disappeared.

His skepticism was clear. "You don't think I deserve to be upset?"

"No, I don't. Maybe at first, but not now."

Now that she was in for a penny, she might as well be in for a pound. He waited for her to continue.

"I don't really know your grandfather, but from what I've seen he's a wonderful person. Let me tell you, if I were in your shoes getting a paid year off, I wouldn't be complaining. I'd be booking tickets to Paris, and following that, Rome. I've never had a real vacation. So having one year to do whatever I wanted, without any limits, would be a dream. Yet you mock the gift he gave you."

He sputtered, amazed by her attack. "I like to work."

She pushed her plate away. "So do I. But work doesn't make me happy. It's a means to an end, not all that I am. My entire existence isn't based on this job."

"I would disagree. You've already indicated how much you need this position and how much financial stability it's bringing you."

"So? That doesn't mean I couldn't be happy doing something else. If I won the lottery, I don't know if I'd stay in business. If I could trade places with you I would, but I can't. I'm here to do a job.

"You know, Chase, your whole life has been a gift, but you don't seem satisfied with what you have. I don't know if you *can* be satisfied."

"Let me tell you, there are many times I've been satisfied," he countered. "And I haven't been the only one, either."

Her face colored at his brash and bold words. His crass humor showed that he hadn't really changed his playboy ways. When cornered, he relied on his top weapon: sex appeal.

"That's not what I meant and you know it," she retorted, crossing her arms over her chest, mimicking his earlier body language. "Unlike you, I don't let my hormones rule my mind." *Or my heart.*

His mouth curled into what could be best described as a Rhett Butler smile. "You should try it sometime. Might do you a world of good."

And with that, the upper hand was Chase's. Refusing to discuss her love life, Miranda pulled her plate toward her and ate some of the turkey sandwich.

However, his words hung in the air between them. She couldn't keep quiet. "You know, I find your insinuation rather insulting."

His blond eyebrows rose. "What?"

She lowered her voice to a whisper. "That having sex might do me a world of good."

"It would do *me* a world of good," Chase replied, popping another French fry into his mouth as if he didn't have a care in the world.

She suddenly had a memory of his mouth on hers, and she wet her lips with her tongue.

"Look, can I say something without you running back to my grandfather and filing sexual harassment charges against me?" he asked.

"I don't know," she said, fascinated with the movement of his mouth. Chase McDaniel had to be a walking pheromone—he rattled her senses and stripped away her usual rigid self-control.

"I'll risk it. I'm leaving town anyway. After this weekend you won't see me again for at least a year."

He leaned forward in his seat and placed his elbows on the table. She found herself waiting for his words. They came quickly and with force. "I've wanted you from the first moment I saw you."

CHASE WATCHED MIRANDA'S reaction to his words. Her eyes widened and her mouth formed a silent *O*. Her face flushed, the rosy color only making her more beautiful. He swallowed. Damn, but he wanted to make love to her. He wanted to cut through the pretense between them and get down to the basics, where there would be nothing but the truth. Sex between them would be phenomenal.

"Okay, you're right, I'm ungrateful. But why shouldn't I be? The most fascinating woman I've met in a long time comes into my life right when I have to leave. Fate's timing sucks."

"You can't mean that," she said, and Chase could almost see the walls she constantly surrounded herself with rising as she regrouped.

He found himself wanting to shake some emotion out of her, make her admit the physical connection between them. "I don't have any reason to mince words. I'm not some jerk who needs a thrill. I'm attracted to you. I thought we'd established that."

"I thought we'd also agreed that this past weekend wasn't to be brought up," she countered. "It was a mistake."

To hell with dumb declarations. He didn't have time for silliness. "First of all, I'm not playing that game. None of it was a mistake. I kissed you because I wanted to. Both times. And believe me, I enjoyed every minute."

Her face reddened further. "You gave me your word that we would pretend nothing happened, and start over."

He shook his head. They were way past that point. They were also adults, not teenagers. "I think I said I'd try. Who knows? I don't really remember what I said. What I do recall is how the moonlight reflected off your hair and how your lips felt on mine. Exquisite."

She gasped at his compliment, but Chase took no

comfort in the fact that he'd shocked her. That hadn't been his intent. Mostly, he'd wanted to clear the air. End the farce.

He glanced up to see the waitress approaching. Maybe it was a good thing she was arriving to check on their meals. He'd never been this blatant before. He was acting out of character. No woman had ever gotten the best of Chase McDaniel. No woman had ever gotten under his skin, not since those first crushes in high school that turned all boys into useless, gibbering mush.

This was different. He was no longer a floundering teenager, but a man who knew what he wanted.

And he wanted Miranda Craig.

Chapter Six

Miranda wasn't certain how she made it through the rest of lunch, much less the next few days. Being around Chase was like walking a tightrope.

Not that he mentioned anything about wanting her again. Once he'd stated his feelings, he'd withdrawn. The business facade had dropped into place, and Chase continued as if nothing had happened.

They'd finished lunch in an odd silence punctuated only by meaningless small talk. In their subsequent work meetings he'd glanced at her, but more as if looking through her than really seeing her. The sense that she'd lost something she hadn't known she wanted was profound.

By Thursday afternoon, she was wired so tightly that when he popped into her office at three o'clock she practically jumped out of her skin.

"Have you checked your e-mails?" he asked without preamble.

"Not since one." She'd been preparing reports since then.

"Didn't think so." He stood in her doorway, with his white shirtsleeves pushed up so that golden-blond hair was visible on his tan forearms. "My grandfather e-mailed an hour and a half ago."

"Oh." Miranda double-clicked an icon on her computer. Normally she checked e-mails at the top of every hour, but since she'd been trying to focus on her reports, she'd kept the program closed.

"Whatever this is, I guess it's important if you walked down here to tell me about it."

He folded his arms. "No. I figured you hadn't read it, or you'd have already found me."

"Okay," Miranda said slowly, opening her in-box. She had thirteen new messages. The one from Leroy McDaniel was near the top. She opened it and found it wasn't even addressed to her, but rather to Chase and copied to her.

She scanned the contents. It seemed that Leroy wanted Chase to bring Miranda with him when he drove up to the lake Friday night. Leroy also intended to take them to dinner Saturday, so they should plan to head back on Sunday once they'd formalized final details of the transition.

"So we're going to the lake," she said.

He watched her closely. "Yes. You'll get your first experience bringing up the paperwork. It's usually my job. Each Friday I take Leroy what he's missed."

No one had told her about this. It figured. She'd hoped to try to relax this weekend. "You do this every week?"

"It's part of my job."

She sensed his irritation. This was one more thing she was usurping.

"So are we riding up together?"

"Normally I go alone."

She deliberately shrugged. Chase needed to deal

with the fact that he was going on sabbatical. "When do we leave?"

"So you're okay with this?" he asked, straightening.

"Why wouldn't I be?"

He moved to stand in front of her desk. "You've been walking on eggshells since Tuesday."

"Me? Hardly." She leaned back and laced her fingers together. "If you're expecting some big drama, you're in the wrong place. It's part of *my* job. You're to show me the ropes. I can handle it."

He rolled his shoulders, the cool, disinterested mask he'd worn since lunch Tuesday falling back into place. "Great, then we leave tomorrow at two. Dinner's casual, so pack accordingly."

With that, he left. Miranda loosened her hands and drummed her fingertips on her desk. She wanted to scream. How did Chase do it? How did he just turn on and off like that?

He was like a stealth bomber, arriving quietly, attacking without warning and dropping an announcement that shook her to the core. Then he'd disappear as if nothing had happened, leaving her to deal with the emotional fallout.

The worst part was that he was treating her exactly how she'd asked him to—but now everything had changed. He'd told her how he felt about her, which was like kicking open Pandora's box.

Miranda pounded her fist on her desk. Darn the man!

She reached for her phone and dialed a number she knew by heart.

Walter picked up on the second ring. "Ready to quit yet?" he joked once she'd said hello.

"No. I'm headed back to the lake, though."

"Ah, bringing Leroy his stuff."

"Yes." Even Walter knew. Miranda suspected Chase had deliberately neglected to tell her until the e-mail arrived.

"During the summer Leroy works from the lake. Chase goes up on Friday nights, spends Saturday morning with him and then is free to do what he wishes," Walter told her.

"We're staying the whole weekend. Something about the transition."

"Then relax and enjoy yourself."

"I just wish I'd had a heads-up. So much about this company isn't written down anywhere. It's in one of the McDaniels' heads. Or some sort of tradition that everyone knows about but me."

"You'll learn. You're lucky you got out of here when you did, by the way. The board hasn't even looked for my replacement. They're going to use someone from within instead on an interim basis. Did you see the news? BevMart made an offer to buy us out. The stock jumped yesterday as speculators scrambled to get on the bandwagon."

"I guess we'll be watching here, since McDaniel's distribution contract is up for renewal next year. I've already learned we have a team in place investigating other options."

"See, you're catching on. Hang in there. I have faith in you. Call me anytime."

Miranda replaced the phone receiver. It had been good to hear Walter's voice. She missed him. He'd always been just down the hall. It made her a little sad to realize they'd never work together again.

She surveyed her office. She'd spent lunch yesterday personalizing her space. She'd hung her diplomas, put her pictures on the shelves. She'd added a few potted plants to the windowsill. Even her apartment was starting to feel like home, but her life didn't seem as calm and serene as her surroundings.

Around quitting time she realized she had no idea who was driving to the lake. She assumed Chase was, but as her first day's lunch had shown, assumptions were something you didn't make around Chase McDaniel. She opened her e-mail.

LEROY SHUFFLED THROUGH the great room early Friday morning, a cup of black coffee in his hand. The rising sun shimmered off the water, and outside the windows, the lake came to life as night receded.

He hadn't slept well. Instead of enjoying a sound sleep, he'd been thinking about the situation with Chase and Miranda, who were due to arrive around dinnertime.

Leroy had woken up feeling all of his eighty years.

A month ago he'd been so certain this had been the right decision. Not that he'd come to doubt Miranda's competency. Even Chase had grudgingly admitted yesterday that she was perfect for the job.

But Leroy knew that nothing was ever simple with Chase. His grandson was one of those deep men. Oh sure, he seemed like the frivolous, self-centered type on the surface, but Leroy knew better. Chase might have run through women like water, but he had a steadfast soul and a pure heart. He was one of those men's men, the kind you wanted fighting by your side. He was intensely loyal, almost to a fault. He just hadn't found what he was looking for yet.

Leroy wanted so much for Chase to be happy. His grandson had been simply existing, going through the motions, for several years. He needed this time off to find himself.

But in the back of his mind, Leroy couldn't help worrying that he might have made a terrible mistake and hurt Chase in a way he'd never intended.

CHASE AND MIRANDA reached Lone Pine Lake around 5:00 p.m. Amazingly, the drive hadn't been that bad. Although she'd been physically aware of him the entire time, for the most part Chase had left her alone to read her book. Conversation had been minimal, and mostly regarding the scenery.

When they stepped out of the SUV, she noticed that Chase's tension melted away. His eyebrows rose when he saw her staring. "What?"

"Nothing. You just seem more relaxed, and we haven't even gotten the luggage out yet."

"This is where I hang my hat," he said, popping the tailgate.

"Meaning?"

"This is where I decompress. It's that way for my whole family. Maybe it's the air or the serenity of the water. Like you said last weekend, you could sit and look out at the lake for hours. You'll probably get the chance."

"I'm too keyed up to relax," she admitted. She'd kissed him here. Her body remembered, even if her brain declared the best kiss of her life off-limits.

"You will. You'll find this place changes your perspective. You'll have lots of opportunities to hang out in the great room, since you're staying above the kitchen."

"I'm not in the cottage?"

He shook his head. "No. Both are occupied. A lot of guests come and go over the summer. My grandmother's sister is staying in one for a season. She prefers to keep her own company, though, so you probably won't meet her. My uncle Harvey and his wife are also here for three weeks. Harvey's my grandfather's younger brother. He's a lawyer."

"Oh, I remember seeing him at the party. We weren't introduced." She and Chase toted their luggage into the lodge and Chase set his on the kitchen floor.

"Let me take those from here." He reached for her carry-on bag and opened the door that led upstairs. Miranda followed him.

She'd seen the room on her first visit. Set into the rafters, the space was like an A-frame, with four dormer windows on one side and a fifth on the opposite wall, filling the room with light.

"Your bathroom is in here," Chase said, showing her a room immediately off the landing that was only large enough for a shower, toilet and pedestal sink. "Feel free to use the armoire for your clothes."

"Okay," she replied, taking her suitcase from him and rolling it to a stop by the double bed. Unlike the front bedrooms, which looked out over the lake, her room had a view of the meadow where Leroy's party had been held. The sun was still high in the sky, and she would have a fantastic view of the sunset.

"Take some time to freshen up and then meet me in, say, thirty minutes?"

"That sounds fine."

Chase's footsteps thudded as he went downstairs, and Miranda sank into the rocking chair. It was a lovely room. She looked at the small table next to her, where on a shelf below, three ancient books waited for someone to pick them up.

She obliged, and opened the first. Inside was the inscription "To my darling Heidi on our fifth anniversary." Leroy had scrawled his signature after the word *Love*. Miranda closed the book and pressed it to her chest, hands folded protectively over the cover. She knew enough McDaniel history to understand how much Leroy had adored his wife.

What would it be like to be loved like that? To be wanted only for yourself?

The only times she'd experienced true passion in a kiss had been in the boathouse and on the dock with Chase. Probably not a good idea to go too near the water this visit!

She replaced the book, changed into casual clothes and made her way to the great room.

"That's a bad habit of yours," she said as she walked into the room.

Chase swiveled around. He was sitting in one of the mission chairs that faced the lake. "What is?"

"Always being early."

He shrugged. "Can't help it. I'm not one of those men who likes to primp."

Of course not, Miranda thought. He was blessed with natural good looks.

He motioned to the chair next to him, and she sat. The leather wrapped around her, drawing her in. On the lake, two sailboats raced by, the water glimmering in the early evening sun. The man next to her was the only reason Miranda couldn't relax.

He'd changed out of his business clothes, and was now wearing boat shoes without socks, Dockers shorts and a polo shirt. He'd kicked his feet up on the windowsill and stretched out.

She dragged her eyes away from his well-muscled legs, and finally found her voice. "Is your grandfather joining us soon?"

"Nope," Chase said easily. "He went over to the cottage to have dinner with Harvey. He made dinner reservations for us, though, and insisted we follow his directives."

She glanced down at the pedal pushers and short-sleeve sweater she wore. Dinner alone with Chase? It sounded as if she'd been fixed up on a blind date. But that was ridiculous. Leroy wouldn't do something like that. This was business. "Okay," she said slowly.

"We're going to the country club. Come on." Chase rose to his feet and she did the same. He opened the front door and led her out to the path. She had an odd sense of déjà vu as they headed toward the boathouse. He walked out onto one of the three Lone Pine docks, where a runabout waited. "Your chariot," he said, hopping into the twenty-foot watercraft.

Miranda hesitated. "You know I've never been in a boat this size." Heck, she'd never been in a canoe.

"You'll love it, as long as you aren't afraid of getting a little wind in your hair." Chase's blue eyes challenged her. "You aren't afraid, are you?"

"Of course not," Miranda retorted, shoving her fears aside.

"Take off your shoes. It'll make climbing in easier."

She passed him her sandals and he set them on the floor of the boat. Then he reached for her hand.

She didn't want to touch him, but had no choice. His grip was tight and secure as he helped her in. She set one foot on the seat, but as her other one landed on the floor, the boat rocked slightly and she fell against Chase.

He caught and steadied her. One hand still held hers, and he trapped it against his chest. He wrapped his other arm around her waist. The magnetic current sizzling between them was unmistakable, and her mouth opened, but no words came out.

Chase loosened his grip and guided her to the seat next to the driver's. "That's your spot, unless you want to sit up front."

"No, this is good," she said. Staying behind the windshield seemed safer, even if she'd be sitting far too close to Chase. Her body quivered. She couldn't deny the physical effect he had on her.

Chase was the proverbial walk on the wild side. She'd stayed on the straight and narrow her whole life.

He tempted her because he represented the fun she'd never had. His innate sexiness was decadent and guaranteed to please.

Yet, like eating too much dessert, she'd have regrets. But would she regret even more not indulging?

"Get ready. We'll be off in a minute."

She sat down, marveling at the ease with which Chase hopped out of the boat, untied the ropes and soon had the craft motoring away from the dock. Once out on open water, they quickly reached cruising speed. The up-and-down motion was at first scary, and then oddly welcome as her fear was replaced with adrenaline.

Being out on the lake was exhilarating. Freeing. If she'd only known! How much of life had she missed?

"Like it?" Chase shouted.

"Love it," Miranda said, scooting forward so she could see over the windshield. The opposite shore was coming into better view; the golf course was visible on the hillside, as were the docks at the base.

Chase cut the engine speed to idle and soon had the boat tied up. He disembarked, and Miranda handed him her sandals. This time, as he helped her out, she didn't falter. She slid her feet back into her shoes and ran her fingers through her hair.

A golf cart waited at the shore, and they used it to get to the clubhouse. "Hey, I see cars," Miranda said as they reached the parking lot.

"It's faster traveling over by boat," Chase replied, parking the golf cart next to some others. "And more fun. You enjoyed it, didn't you?"

"I did."

He grinned and her heart skipped a beat. "I took a risk that you would. I think I have you pegged."

She drew herself up. "I doubt that."

His cheeky grin said it all. The fun-loving Chase was back. "I don't. Besides, you're in *my* world now. Let's go eat."

BY THE END OF DINNER, Miranda had finally relaxed, and she'd met most of the people who lived around the lakeshore. The country club was definitely the place to be on a Friday night. She'd been surprised to learn that the club was public—anyone could use the golf course and enjoy the restaurant. Many of the folks she'd met had been at Leroy's birthday party, and those who hadn't were quick to accept her as a new McDaniel employee.

"So you don't bring dates here, either?" she teased as she and Chase walked back to the dock, opting to leave the golf cart behind after they'd finished their meal. The sun was dipping below the treetops by the time they left. Although the sky wasn't totally dark, low voltage lights illuminated the walkway.

"No. I've never brought a girlfriend to the lake."

"Really?" That surprised her.

He shrugged. "This is my space. I guess I've never found the woman I wanted to share it with."

Again he helped her into the boat. This time Miranda was sure of her footing, but touching him still sent a tingle to her toes. She told herself it was the two glasses of wine she'd had. Or maybe a residual sugar high from the decadent chocolate cake she'd eaten.

"So would you like a tour? I think night's the best time to be on the water," Chase said once they'd gotten under way. "Lone Pine is actually part of a chain of lakes. To the north is Balsam Lake. It's smaller and rounder." He made the decision for her. "I'll show you. It's not far."

Miranda settled back against the seat as they chugged along. Unlike earlier in the day, he'd now grown chatty.

Chase had had only one glass of wine with dinner, so Miranda knew the reason wasn't alcohol. Rather, she suspected it was because he loved the area. He knew every inch of lakeshore, and pointed out various houses and told her about their histories and current occupants.

She was laughing at one of his accounts as they came to a bridge across a narrows. "That's Highway A," he told her. "If you hadn't stopped that day, you would eventually have crossed this bridge."

"I must have turned around right before I reached it."

"Probably." He decreased speed, and they coasted through the channel, which was twelve feet wide at most. The bridge was about fifty feet above their heads as they puttered beneath.

After they got through the bottleneck, the lake opened up. However, unlike Lone Pine, Balsam Lake was egg-shaped, and only a half mile across and a mile long. A few houses sat high on the hills surrounding it, their docks far below and many sets of stairs away. Chase brought the boat to a halt in the center of the lake, turned off the engine and floated.

"Hear how quiet it is."

Miranda listened. It was as if they'd entered another world. The lake water was dark and deep, and the sun had disappeared, leaving only the final reddish tints of twilight. The sounds of humanity had ceased, but all around her the song of nature came to life as nocturnal animals and insects came out to play.

The night spoke of romance. It was heavy with solace and peace, and the undercurrent of something permanent and magical.

And it felt as if all those things she had been looking for her entire life could be found simply by turning to the man who sat next to her, as lost in the moment as she was.

All she had to do was say his name, and yet Miranda knew no words should be spoken. They had no future.

As if emphasizing that depressing point, a mosquito buzzed by, and Chase restarted the engine. "That's our cue," he said. "If they start to bite, there's bug spray in the glove box in front of you. But we should be going fast enough to keep them away."

"Thank you," Miranda said, as they made their way back to Lone Pine Lake.

"For what?"

"For sharing. I've never been anywhere like this."

"I used to do a lot of night fishing. It's peaceful. During the day Balsam's the best place to water-ski. It's a well-kept secret."

"I've never tried any water sports."

"Really? You'll have to let me teach you how to ski sometime."

"I doubt I'll be skiing when I'm here. Just bringing your grandfather his work and leaving the next morning."

"Then you'll be missing out." Chase pushed on the throttle as they hit open water. He clicked a button and the boat's running lights came on. Darkness had settled, and all along the lakeshore house lights flickered.

"I'll take you to see the rest of the lake tomorrow," he said as he turned the boat toward the Lone Pine docks. In the distance Miranda could see the lodge sitting on the hillside like a majestic queen, the glow from her windows welcoming. A lump formed in her throat and she shivered. This was Chase's home.

Not hers. As much as she'd like to, she didn't belong here.

He saw her shiver. "Cold?"

"I'm fine." The temperature had dropped, but her chill was from the sad feelings overtaking her. Under any other circumstances she and Chase could probably have been friends. Perhaps even lovers. Maybe more.

He was like no other man she'd ever met. They had fun when they were together. He'd wanted her once. They'd kissed. Twice.

She would probably find the love that was missing from her life if only they'd met in another time and place, where outside forces didn't dictate their roles, and he didn't despise her for taking his job. She'd coveted his position and his lifestyle, and fate had handed them to her at his expense.

But she'd learned one thing tonight. Despite what people said, you couldn't have it all.

From the great room windows, Leroy watched as Chase moored the boat. The two looked as if they'd had fun.

"Are we working tonight?" Miranda asked, when she and Chase entered the lodge.

"No. Tonight's about relaxing," Leroy replied. "We'll start at eight-thirty tomorrow, over breakfast. So how was dinner?"

"Mr. and Mrs. Simmons send birthday greetings and asked me to say they're sorry they missed your party. They were in Hawaii. But they want you to know you're to come to their Fourth of July bash just like every year," Chase said.

"Wouldn't miss it," Leroy said. He turned to Miranda. "So did you like the country club? It's modeled after Saint Andrew's in Scotland."

"I did. The food was terrific. And afterward Chase showed me Balsam Lake."

Ah. That's where they'd been. Although, as Leroy assessed his grandson's body language, he could tell nothing had happened.

"There aren't any fish in that lake, either," Leroy grumbled, continuing to observe the pair. He usually despised the women Chase dated, but Miranda just might be perfect for him. The signs were all there.

"We McDaniels aren't very lucky with fishing," Chase explained.

"Never even seen a keeper," Leroy added, keeping the small talk going while watching Chase for signs that he was interested in Miranda. His grandson had mastered the poker face. Miranda was easier to read, and her expressions revealed a lot. "I've arranged for us to eat on the big island tomorrow. Harvey and Laverne are coming, too."

"That sounds nice," Miranda said politely.

"The lodge there is the only property on the lake older than this one. It's now a resort. You can see their boathouse from here. I'll show it to you up close tomorrow," Chase offered.

"They've done a good job of restoration," Leroy said. "We were worried for a while that it might get demolished for condos or something. Places like this need to be preserved."

"I agree." Miranda stood there for a moment. "So we're meeting at eight-thirty?"

Chase nodded.

"Then, if you both don't mind, I'm going to turn in. Good night." And with that, she was gone. Leroy noticed the way Chase's eyes followed her. So the boy did like her a little.

"How was your dinner?" Chase asked.

"Great. Laverne made meat loaf. Sent me the leftovers for lunch." He loved meat loaf, especially the next day in a sandwich. "So you took her to Balsam?" he prodded.

"She'd never been out on a boat before tonight. She loved it."

"Unlike the floozies you date."

"I never brought anyone here," Chase snapped.

Leroy suppressed a chuckle. Chase was testy. He was more affected by Miranda than he let on. "Your previous women were more the yacht type, and we don't own one of those. Too big and fancy for my britches. People shouldn't show off just because they can."

"I agree. We've had this discussion many times. You aren't trying to push Miranda on me, are you?"

Leroy realized he was entering dangerous waters. He wasn't good at matchmaking, that had been Heidi's forte. He decided to try another tactic.

"No, but Miranda's good people. Has her priorities straight. Did you know she's putting her sister through college?"

"She mentioned that when we had lunch Tuesday."

So Chase was playing this one close to the chest. "Her dedication to her family was one of the things that most impressed me about her. She puts everyone else before herself."

"She's a saint," Chase agreed, rolling his eyes.

"You've done a lot worse," Leroy pointed out.

"What do you mean by that?"

Oh, boy. He'd backed himself into a corner. For a shrewd businessman, Leroy had really botched this. "Nothing. Just the ramblings of an old man. Forget it."

"Grandpa…"

Leroy began shuffling off to his bedroom. At eighty, his legs didn't move as fast as they used to. "Gotta turn in. It's late. See you in the morning."

With a wave over his shoulder, he left Chase alone, standing in the great room.

CHASE WATCHED his grandfather go, and hoped that turning eighty hadn't made the old man senile. For Leroy to insinuate that he should date Miranda… That certainly wasn't the Leroy Chase knew.

He busied himself turning off lights. The great room became pitch-black, and it took awhile for his eyes to become accustomed enough to see the outlines of furniture. He made it through the room by habit more than sight, and soon was up in his bedroom.

Two hours later he was still wide-awake, with Miranda dominating his thoughts. He'd wanted to kiss her when they'd stopped to enjoy the solitude of Balsam Lake. He'd sensed she might be willing. But he'd only be in Chenille for a few more days, and she wasn't the one-night-stand type. Chase threw off the covers and went to the window.

Movement caught his eye, and he sucked in a breath. He couldn't believe it.

There Miranda was, out on the dock, just like last weekend.

He didn't hesitate. He grabbed his shoes and left, sleep forgotten.

Chapter Seven

"It's a wicked full moon, isn't it," Chase said as he walked down to the dock. Unlike last weekend, Miranda didn't jump. She'd heard him coming.

Part of her had thought to flee, but that idea flickered out quickly. Deep down, she'd hoped he would come. Her intuition and her desire had wished for him, and here he was, as if she'd conjured him up.

He dropped to the planking beside her and kicked off his leather shoes before dangling his feet over the water. "No wonder we couldn't sleep. It's gorgeous out here. Even better than earlier."

The full moon illuminated the sky and the water, creating a river of light.

"We should take the boat out," Chase suggested.

When he said that, Miranda's pulse quickened. She hadn't really thought this plan through. Heck, she hadn't been thinking at all, but acting more on impulse, which was why she was out here wearing shorts and a T-shirt. "Sitting on the dock is fine."

"No, come on. Indulge me." He reached into his short pockets and withdrew a key fob. "This is one of my favorite things and not something I share with most people."

That swayed her and she decided to take a risk. "Okay."

This time they headed south, toward the middle of the lake and the big island. She could see the lights of the resort's boathouse in the distance.

"The big island creates a wonderful illusion," Chase told her. "It looks as if it's a shoreline in itself, making the lake appear smaller than it really is. Most of the lake is behind the island."

"I feel miles from anywhere," she commented, glancing around. The runabout didn't have headlights, only the bow and stern safety lights. Far off, near the eastern shore, another boat had dropped anchor.

"They're probably fishing," Chase said. He killed the motor and let their craft drift.

"You aren't going to lower the anchor?"

"This is the deepest part of the lake, fifty-three feet. And unlike a river, there's no current. We'll just see where the wind takes us. We're far enough out that we're not in any danger, and other boats can see our lights."

Chase turned to her, shifting his legs into the center aisle. "I love being out on the water at night. I can't really even tell you why. I just do."

Silence descended as he let the magical ambience carry him away. Miranda's eyes had grown accustomed to the moonlight and she simply sat and listened.

Waves lapped against the fiberglass hull with a gentle *thuwump*. She could hear whip-poor-wills calling. Somewhere an owl hooted, the sound carrying across the water. The boat rocked gently, a soothing motion. Tension drained from her.

"Wow," she said. "I see what you mean."

"I'm glad. Boating's got to call you. While they like it, no one else in my family loves being on the water as much as I do. My grandfather won't get in a boat at all if he can help it."

"Really?" Miranda's legs tangled with his in the space between the seats as she faced him.

"He loves to look at the water, but he's petrified of being out on it. He'll have to get on the ferry tomorrow to go to dinner. That shows how important you are to him."

"Was he always like that?"

"No. He was in a sailboat accident when he was in his twenties. No one got hurt, but he was finished with boating."

"Yet your family has all these boats."

Chase took her hand and ran his thumb over her sensitive palm. "He made sure we weren't afraid. Although none of us like small planes."

"Because of your parents."

"My dad loved to fly. But he made a basic beginner's mistake, and it cost him and my mother their lives. They never should have been out in that weather, even though he was certified for instruments and—"

"Shh." Miranda freed her right hand and reached forward to put a finger on his lips. "It's too beautiful out here for regrets or sorrow."

"It is," he whispered, his breath hot on her fingertip. She started to pull away, but Chase wrapped his hand around her wrist. "I like the way that felt." He replaced her finger. "See?"

His lips were soft, and she shivered as a wave of desire washed over her.

A bass boat cruised by, about thirty feet away, and the runabout rocked as the wake reached it. Chase used the opportunity to kiss Miranda's fingertips. He slid his mouth up to her knuckle, using his tongue to encircle the digit in a gentle caress.

His gaze locked on to hers, and like a moth drawn to a flame, she couldn't pull away. Heat flared in every pore.

"I want to kiss you," he said.

She wanted nothing more. What could one kiss hurt? Everything she'd worked for.

But his sensual suckling of her fingers had her quivering, and when Chase's lips moved to hers she couldn't resist indulging in the sweetness of his kiss.

She lost track of time as the kiss swept her away. Then coolness descended as Chase moved to start the engine, and Miranda realized they'd drifted close to one of the tiny, uninhabited islands, a piece of ground probably not even a sixth of an acre in size. Chase eased the boat away from the danger of running aground.

"Want to drive?"

"Is it safe?" she asked, ignoring the immediate *Yes!* inside her head.

"So long as you don't turn the wheel too sharply, it's like driving a car. Just head toward those lights. That's our dock."

They changed seats and Miranda gripped the steering wheel. "It's not going to jump out of your hands," Chase chided. She forced her fingers to loosen. He leaned over her shoulder. "That's the throttle. Press forward to go faster. Pull back to ease up."

The top of the throttle was about the size of a bar of soap and fit perfectly under her palm. She eased the lever forward and the boat picked up speed. As they cut through the water she couldn't help herself. "I'm driving!" she shouted.

He laughed. "You are. Turn left. Gently. Not too fast."

Miranda did, and the boat turned. She drove for about five minutes, until they came close to the Lone Pine docks. "Put it in neutral," Chase instructed.

He again took the driver's seat, steering the boat in. He hopped out and tied up, and then reached to help Miranda.

She placed her hand in his, as she'd been doing all day. But when she set foot on the dock, he pulled her to him, into an embrace. His arms tightened around her.

"Fun?" he asked, raising one hand to brush away a loose tendril of hair.

"I had the best time," she replied. Her body trembled from the excitement of driving the boat and the giddy pleasure of being pressed up against Chase's body. "The lake was wonderful. Thank you. You were—"

His impatient kiss swallowed the rest of her words, which probably weren't important, anyway. She leaned into him and the passion flaring between them spoke for itself.

This was what she wanted. She desired him as much as he desired her. His kiss changed tempo, but he didn't break contact. Instead, what had been urgent softened. He touched her jaw with his free hand. He seemed intent on exploration, on making sure the moment stretched. Almost as if he was memorizing the taste and texture of her lips.

"So perfect," he murmured, the hand on her back guiding her still closer.

She had no idea how her legs managed to hold her weight. Her knees felt like jelly. She clung to Chase, molding herself to the hard planes of his hips and chest. The soft hairs of his legs tickled her thighs. She could sense every inch of him—especially that part revealing exactly what kissing her did to him.

Then his lips left hers, and he eased back and touched the edge of her mouth with the pad of his thumb, a gentle caress.

"I'm sorry," he said.

Miranda froze. It was as if someone had dumped a bucket of ice water over her head. Her shoulders stiffened and she cringed. How many times had she heard those words? "I'm sorry" had been Manuel's only response after using her.

Hearing the words *I'm terribly sorry* hadn't brought her parents back.

I'm sorry was like *but.* The words following were never good and never said anything that really helped. *I'm sorry* was simply a way to ease a person's guilt, a way for him to make himself feel better.

She'd put herself out there with Chase, taken a chance, and here came the rejection. She steeled herself, waiting for the rest.

"You rattle me. I want you. I've never pretended otherwise. But I don't want you to get the wrong idea. I didn't come down here to seduce you."

Anger and shame bubbled forth as he tarnished what had been a beautiful moment. Miranda hated herself. She'd given in when she shouldn't have. She had to salvage some of her pride, especially when she had read more into the night than he'd intended.

"Look. You told me you wanted me. I'm not some dumb virgin without a clue. I'm not trying to trap you. The kiss was nice, until you went and made a mere kiss more than it was." She stepped away from him.

"That's why I stopped. I got carried away. I don't want you to think I'm trying to take advantage of you, especially given our work situation. I'm returning at the end of my sabbatical, and when I do, I'll be CEO."

Her eyebrows knit together. "A year is a long time. You could change your mind."

"Won't happen. My grandfather promised to make me CEO when I get back. He's a man of his word."

Miranda wrapped her arms protectively around her torso. The night air felt cold, or perhaps the chill came from once again going too far with the wrong man.

"Okay," Chase said when the silence stretched. "Tell me how it plays out. Wait, let me guess. We ignore it. Pretend it didn't happen?"

He smiled then, obviously trying to diffuse the tension with humor.

"I don't think that works anymore. A bad idea on my part," she conceded.

"Whew. Because that wasn't just a notch-on-my-belt kiss. You have to understand that."

"Oh." Learning the kiss had affected Chase softened her toward him.

"Look," he said in a low voice. "There's something between us."

"I know." She dropped her gaze. Chase had turned her emotions into quicksand. "You're leaving."

"Yes. But maybe that's for the best. Perhaps we should get the physical stuff out of our systems. After a year apart, we'll have moved on and be able to work together without distraction. I'll come back and you'll step aside and all will be well."

"You make it sound so simple." Then again, guys did think with their libido.

"It can be. I stopped, not because I didn't want to make love to you, but because I wanted both of us to be on the same page before we did. If we make love, I don't want regrets."

"I agree," she conceded. "You know, sometimes I wish I hadn't taken this job."

He laughed. "No you don't. It's just that you don't let yourself go. Maybe this weekend you could."

Miranda wanted nothing more than to say yes and

let herself experience everything a man with a body like
his could offer.

"It's probably time for bed." She stifled a yawn. "Let
me sleep on this."

"I'll walk you up." Chase saw her to the stairs that
led to her room above the kitchen. Minutes later, she
crawled into bed and lay staring up at the ceiling.

Chase made her long for things best left unknown.
Yet he was a gentleman. If he'd been a cad, he wouldn't
have stopped. That he had was some comfort.

Each kiss, however, made her want more. Kissing
wasn't enough. She was in danger of forgetting a fundamental truth: you can't have it all. And with Chase
determined to be CEO, she never would.

Chapter Eight

"I think that about wraps it up." Leroy set aside the stack of file folders.

Chase checked the time. His grandfather had promised at the start of the business meeting that they'd be finished by lunch, and he'd kept his word.

Leroy's smile widened. "I believe this works, and no more transition is needed. Monday we'll meet with the board and finalize everything."

Chase organized the papers in front of him. Two days from now he would straighten his desk, forward his phone and e-mail and turn off the lights for a year.

"I'm thrilled you've caught on so quickly," Leroy told Miranda. "The board won't have any issue with your taking over for Chase. I'll still be running everything and I can assist you with whatever you don't know."

"Thank you." She bowed her head and stacked her own papers, then slid them inside her briefcase.

"I can't resist my leftover meatloaf from last night, so maybe Chase could take you into Birchwood for lunch. There's not much to eat here, unfortunately, and it's almost time for my siesta."

Leroy rose to his feet and Chase put the file folders into his grandfather's briefcase. This was the last time he and his grandfather would complete this ritual for at least a year. Next weekend Miranda would bring the work Leroy had to address before Monday.

A hard lump formed in Chase's throat, one he couldn't swallow. When he'd expected to be named CEO and take over, he'd planned to spend Saturdays discussing the company with his grandfather. He'd be in charge, but Leroy would be there to help.

Chase had been looking forward to that transition. However, with the definitive click of the briefcase, he fulfilled his last duty, and his obligation to McDaniel ended.

Whatever this year of finding himself was about, it started now.

He glanced at Miranda. She'd done well today. She was perfect for the job. The fact that she fit him perfectly, as well, was something he'd have to forget after this weekend.

"You need to see Birchwood," Leroy was saying.

Chase could tell Miranda didn't necessarily want to go to lunch with him, but since Leroy was insisting she learn the lay of the land, Chase knew she wouldn't refuse.

"I'm ready when you are," he told her, taking advantage of his grandfather's arm twisting. She hadn't said a definite no last night, so there was still the possibility that something could happen between them. He wanted to see where that possibility led. "Say five minutes?"

"Okay." She rose and disappeared into the kitchen.

"You sure you're fine with meatloaf sandwiches?" Chase asked. "We could bring you something back."

Leroy nodded. "I want to take a nap. I tossed and turned last night."

Chase was immediately concerned. "You feeling okay?"

The older man gave a dismissive wave. "Fine. You can't have a perfect sleep every night, especially at my age. This transition has weighed on me, as well."

"I'm going quietly," Chase said.

Leroy's shoulders sagged and his blue eyes didn't sparkle like they usually did. "I know. To be honest, I wish you weren't. It's rather unlike you. I expected you to kick and scream the whole way."

Chase frowned as Leroy walked into the kitchen and opened the refrigerator. His grandfather removed a plastic container. "I'll talk to you later tonight. I'm going to eat in my room. Be sure to show Miranda the sights."

"I will," Chase promised. He couldn't help worrying about his grandfather, who'd been acting odd these past few days. Chase tried to brush the thoughts aside. They'd talk later, as Leroy had said. Miranda was coming downstairs and didn't need to sense any of this stress. Chase met her at the bottom. "Ready?"

"As much as I'll ever be."

BIRCHWOOD WAS TINY—only five blocks wide. But it had a fantastic sandwich shop and Miranda enjoyed her lunch despite the tension between her and Chase.

She tried not to think about their discussion last night, but it was like an elephant in the room—impossible to ignore.

"Still want to go out on the water with me or have we been together enough?" Chase asked on the drive back.

It was boating or reading, and she'd made a poor choice in the book she'd brought. It was supposed to be a thriller, but it always put her to sleep. "I like boating. Do you mind?"

"No. I wouldn't have suggested it otherwise," Chase said. "Do you want to drive?"

Miranda laughed, and some of the tension between them dissipated. "Absolutely."

It turned into an idyllic day. Chase didn't try to kiss her, but focused on teaching her all about boat operation. They toured the entire lake, going behind the big island, where the shoreline's shape resembled the lower half of Africa. Down at the tip, a channel narrower than the one leading to Balsam Lake led to the last lake in the chain, Red Cedar.

"Wow," she said. Not ready to negotiate the shallows there, she let Chase maneuver the runabout through, and suddenly they popped out from under the trees into a rectangular lake not even a thousand feet across at its widest point.

"The entire lake has only four houses on it," Chase said. "This is another good place to water-ski because it has very little boat traffic. And the trees block the wind, making the water as smooth as glass."

Chase returned through the passage, and once back on Lone Pine, opened the throttle, letting the boat cruise at a higher speed. The ride was exhilarating, yet Miranda's excitement slipped away. Tonight was her last night with Chase.

She'd never felt so conflicted. Should she say yes to what could quite possibly be the best sex of her life, or say no and maintain the status quo? Either way, two things didn't change. A year was a long time, and at the end of it, Chase planned to return, stopping her ascent to the top spot.

The last thought rankled so much that she climbed

out of the boat without waiting for his help. She took the rope he tossed her, and looped it over a post, mooring the bow. "Thanks for taking me."

"You're welcome." Chase busied himself securing the stern and putting out the bumpers.

This man, who made her knees weak with a kiss, was leaving for good. Overwhelmed by her feelings, Miranda decided to make a quick escape. "I'll catch you at dinner. I'm going to go clean up and check my e-mails."

"Sure," Chase said.

And with that, she fled.

As much as he wanted to, Chase refused to turn around and eye her sexy backside. He didn't want to watch her walk away from him.

Hell, they were two consenting adults. Maybe he should have made love to her last night instead of being chivalrous. He would have gotten her out of his system. She hadn't been protesting. A year was plenty of time to put any residual awkwardness behind them.

But he wanted her to make the decision. He had to respect her need for space.

He stepped onto the dock. Here he was in paradise and he'd never been so frustrated.

He had some extra tennis shoes in the boathouse. A long run on the treadmill would do him a world of good. He had time to get in at least an hour's workout. Perfect.

Leroy watched as Chase came out of the boathouse. Leroy had woken up from his nap just before their return. He pressed his fingers to his temples. No use.

He was as stressed as his grandson.

It had been easy to see the tension in Chase's shoulders, and his disappearance into the boathouse meant he was running. That's what Chase did to cope. He exercised. He pushed his body to the point of exhaustion. When his parents had died, Chase had also turned his attention to work. He'd focused on his siblings. He'd wanted to know what needed to be done, and then he did it.

Leroy had wanted Chase to yell or scream or rage, or even cry. But he never had, at least not in front of anyone. His siblings had been able to let the tears out. Cecilia had cried herself to sleep for three months.

But Chase always kept his emotions guarded like a fortress. Miranda Craig had cracked his armor; Leroy could tell that much. But Chase was being stoic and chivalrous.

Leroy cursed under his breath and stepped off his sunporch, back into his suite. He wanted his grandson to be alive. To truly feel—and not just some fleeting passion with those women he usually dated. It was as if Chase pursued the wrong type just so he didn't have to emotionally invest himself. That was one reason Leroy had decided on this sabbatical. He wanted Chase to find what was missing in his life. Stripped of work, Chase would have to face himself.

"Damn," Leroy said, hitting the top of his dresser for emphasis. If his wife were around she'd immediately chastise him. Leroy let the memory bring a smile to his lips. It was bittersweet, but he believed he'd see her again. It just wasn't time.

First Leroy had Chase to worry about. At the other end of the house a door slammed, indicating that his grandson had arrived inside. Leroy sank down in his chair. Too bad he couldn't have seen into the future. If he'd known how Miranda would make Chase's skin prickle, Leroy would've hired her years ago, and would never have needed to send his grandson away.

If only Chase would fight to stay…

But family loyalty and doing the right thing came first for Chase. He wouldn't go against Leroy's wishes.

A year was but a grain of sand in the hourglass of time, Leroy reminded himself. Still, he couldn't help second-guessing himself.

THEIR DINNER DESTINATION, Marstall's Lodge Resort, could only be reached by boat. Housed on the twenty-seven acre island in the center of Lone Pine Lake, Marstall's Lodge was a former lumber baron's palatial summer home now open to visitors.

"This place is as old as me," Leroy announced. He'd braved the resort's ferry and walked up the ramp to the main building. "Of course, they've updated it."

"But they preserved it well," Leroy's brother, Harvey, said. He reached out a hand to assist his wife. "I helped them get it on the national historic registry. I'm their lawyer."

"You lived here?" Miranda asked. She'd thought they lived in Florida.

"For a while. Outside Bloomington, Minnesota. I met Laverne one summer after Leroy found this place, and that was the end of Chenille for me."

"We retired to Naples," Laverne explained. "My father was in charge of the construction crew that rehabbed Lone Pine Lodge. It was in pretty bad shape when Leroy bought it."

"We fixed it up right," Leroy said.

The brick walkway brought them to the main doors

of Marstall's Lodge, and they climbed the steps to the stone patio.

Like Lone Pine, the place was made entirely of wood. The logs had been left exposed, including the beams that spanned the peaked ceiling. Light fell from wooden chandeliers that didn't have a hint of crystal. Mounted deer heads lined the walls and the furniture was rustic. The massive stone fireplace reminded Miranda of Lone Pine's, only bigger.

She looked down at her sundress, and mentally sighed. Most people were in casual shirts and pants.

The bell she'd seen earlier, hanging in its wooden tower, sounded, and soon every table in the massive room had filled with guests. The McDaniels' round table for five was comfortable, but Miranda sat next to Chase, whose leg kept brushing against hers. And when she passed him the butter tray their fingers touched, sending a shiver down her spine.

"So, Miranda, tell me a little about yourself," Laverne said. Grateful for the diversion, she told them the edited and condensed version of her history she'd long ago perfected.

"I think it's wonderful that this is your dream job," Laverne stated.

"I agree," Harvey said. "So, Chase, we hear you're taking a vacation. Where are you headed?"

"Think I'll go west. Colorado, Montana, Wyoming, one of those."

"All good choices. You can do some fly-fishing," Harvey said.

"Probably won't catch anything," Leroy teased.

"I might," Chase replied. "Maybe our curse is only for Minnesota lakes."

"Nope. I never catch fish anywhere," Leroy said.

Everyone laughed, and Miranda marveled at the easy way the family got along. She knew Chase was bitter, but he never let it show. She awarded him some brownie points for that. Living at her aunt's had always been tense. Miranda doubted she would handle the family interference as well as he had.

"I can't eat another thing," she protested when the dessert tray came by.

"Take a walk after dinner to work off the calories. You have to take her to the gazebo, Chase," Laverne suggested.

"I doubt Miranda wants a stroll."

Since Chase's leg was pressed up against hers, Miranda thought she might be better off going home and taking a cold shower. "It's okay. Chase has already played tour guide once today."

"The island is gorgeous. You really must see the grounds while you're here," Laverne insisted.

What was it with this family and tours? Miranda started to wonder if there was a conspiracy to get her and Chase alone together.

"Besides, Chase won't mind," Leroy said, as if his statement settled matters.

Miranda knew Chase did mind. He'd grown tense beside her. She had no idea what he was thinking, but the gazebo didn't sound like a safe place for two people trying to keep their hands to themselves.

But he must have realized there was no arguing with the older McDaniels. "I'd be happy to show you," he said. "Shall we forgo dessert?" He was already getting to his feet.

"Don't forget to take a peek at the rose garden, too," Laverne added. "It's on the way."

"I'm sorry you have to keep taking me places,"

Miranda told him as they left the dining hall. "I'm not sure why your grandfather is being so stubborn."

"I think it's because he knows I hit on you once."

She stopped dead. "What?"

Chase took her arm and gently propelled her forward, down a stone walkway through the flower gardens. She was so furious at his admission that she saw nothing but the path ahead. They reached a wrought-iron bridge that covered a ten-foot-wide inlet from the lake.

"The island is really two parts, but the water here is so shallow the only craft that can get through is a canoe. A long time ago it might have been wider, but it's filled in over the years."

"I couldn't care less about canoes. What do you mean, you told him you hit on me?"

Chase shrugged. "He asked. I told him about the first day we met. It's the truth, after all."

"Oh my God." Miranda tried to process the implications as they crossed the bridge. "Don't tell me he's matchmaking."

"Quite possibly. With Leroy you never know."

"I don't believe this. Is that why you keep kissing me?"

Chase paused and put a hand on her arm. "Trust me, my grandfather has no influence over what I want to do with you. And you seem to enjoy it."

She did. Which was the problem. Knowing Leroy knew about her and Chase…it was embarrassing. She didn't want to be seen as unprofessional.

The path changed from stones to gravel and they began walking up hill to the northernmost point, where a square stone structure awaited exploration. The door had long since vanished, as had the glass in the windows, but inside there was a fireplace and a small picnic table.

They were about twenty feet above the lake level but surrounded by trees, which blocked most of the light.

"This is it—the gazebo. There's not much to see, I'm afraid. The view's better from the lawn. Shall we go?"

Miranda wasn't listening. She'd been captivated. Didn't Chase see how perfect this place was? This was where you'd spend lazy summer afternoons with a picnic basket and a book. She went inside and ran her fingers over the weathered stones. She couldn't help herself. The building called to her spirit. "You could really let your imagination run wild in a place like this."

"Yeah," Chase said. He sounded bored.

She whirled to face him, where he stood in the doorway.

"Oh come on. Didn't you ever play make-believe when you were a kid?"

"When I was six."

She planted her hands on her hips. "And you tell me I never relax. I could bring a book here and hide out. This is the perfect place for make-believe. If *I* was six I'd dream of princes and such."

"We're not six," Chase pointed out.

"So? That doesn't make it wrong. All girls want to be princesses at some point in their lives. Even if we plan on saving ourselves."

He took a step forward. "Guys don't dream about being princes."

"So what would you be? If you were six?"

He thought for a second. "Guys would rather be pirates or swashbucklers. Cowboys maybe. Something boisterous and rowdy. Rough-and-tumble."

"Then this could be where you hide your pirate loot.

Or it could be your lookout. I bet in the winter you can see the whole lake."

"In the winter the lake is frozen solid. People bring out their ice huts and fish. It's not that glamorous."

She ignored his derision. "Even better. You could pretend they were your army, out camping. I used to make up stories all the time for my little sister, every night before she went to bed. She'd probably like this old building as much as I do. She collects antiques."

Chase shoved his hands into his pockets. "You'll have to invite her for a visit. Leroy will let you bring a guest, and I'm sure she'll love the lake."

"I will, if she's not too busy. Her schedule rivals mine. She's even more determined than I am to make something of herself."

Chase shifted his weight. "So tell me, what would a pirate do if this was his hideaway?"

"Count his treasure?" she answered, turning her back as she checked out graffiti someone had etched into the picnic table, so small you almost couldn't see it unless you were looking for it: *L.L. + H.M. Forever.*

"Do you think I could be a pirate?" Chase stepped closer and her body reacted to the undercurrent in his words. He was right behind her. She turned around.

He was hotter than both Johnny Depp and Orlando Bloom in the *Pirates of the Caribbean* trilogy, and unlike the characters they played, Chase was very real. And male. And, as always, larger than life. She had the urge to unbutton his shirt and run her hands over his chest. "Would you plunder things?"

"Oh yeah." His voice was low and husky, his gaze locked on to her lips. Her skin prickled with heightened anticipation. They were totally alone, where no one could see or find them. "If I were a pirate there are certainly things I'd like to plunder."

She sucked in a breath. All Chase had to do was insinuate, and she wanted him. If he kissed her, she'd be a goner. She knew she should resist, but couldn't bring herself to do so.

"Like what?" she asked, giving him the opening they both wanted.

"This." He dipped his head, his mouth finding hers. The kiss mesmerized Miranda, and Chase pulled her to him, hauling her up and seating her on the picnic table so he could stand between her legs.

His arms slid around her waist and his tongue dipped inside. She threaded her fingers into his hair as he moved one hand to her breast. He ran his thumb across the tight bud, and she wished they didn't have so many clothes on.

"I want you," Chase growled, and as he pressed between her thighs, she could feel how much. He shifted, rubbing against her.

"Oh." All she had to do was say yes.

He was still kissing her, and the light faded further, casting the gazebo in shadows. She felt heady and sexy. Wanton. The only place she'd ever made love was in a bed.

He hiked her dress up and moved his hand beneath the scrap of lace that was her panties. He continued to kiss her as his fingers worked to give her the release her body craved. He held her tight with one arm as she bucked and whimpered, then finally shattered.

Afterwards, he readjusted her clothing, kissed her gently and held her as her breathing slowly returned to normal. "Good fantasy?"

. She didn't have words. She didn't need any. She simply nodded. Tonight had only just begun.

THE SUN WAS ALMOST GONE when Chase and Miranda returned from their walk.

Leroy sipped his decaffeinated coffee as he rested in one of the Adirondack chairs on the back lawn, chatting with Harvey and Laverne. The area was well lit by citronella torches, making it an ideal place to watch the sunset.

"Sit a spell," he said as Chase and Miranda approached. "The ferry isn't back yet."

Miranda sank into a chair as the final slivers of gold dipped below the horizon.

"How was your walk?" Laverne asked.

"Great," she answered.

"Do they still have that old picnic table up there? Harvey carved our initials in it long ago."

Miranda's face colored. "It's still there."

Leroy resisted a chuckle. Something had happened, he was sure of it. Then he sobered. Chase had disappeared into Marstall's Lodge. Maybe whatever had occurred hadn't been a good thing…

Heidi would have known what to do. Leroy wished he had her wisdom in matters of the heart.

The bell rang, signaling the ferry's arrival.

Leroy rose to his feet. "Time to go."

BY THE TIME the group returned to Lone Pine, Miranda should have been calm. No one could tell what she and Chase had just done. And she wanted more. She was damned if she made love to Chase and damned if she didn't. But her answer was yes.

She'd risk it.

She studied the lines of his face, watched him kiss his great-aunt and shake his great-uncle's hand. In a year, Chase might come home from his sabbatical married.

Miranda gazed at the full moon, visible through the great room windows. One night. Tonight was all they had, and no man had ever made her feel the way he did.

Would it make her less of a woman or an executive if she gave in to her desires, the ones she'd been fighting ever since she met him?

She grasped at the first idea that came to mind once Leroy left the room. "I want to take the boat out. How about we go change and meet each other on the dock in ten minutes?"

Chase studied her. "Okay."

Miranda's feet had never moved so fast. She hurried to her room, changed and took a blanket from the armoire. Then she went into the kitchen and grabbed a bottle of merlot from a cabinet. She found a plastic trash bag, wrapped the wine in the blanket and stuffed both inside. Then she tossed in two plastic cups and a corkscrew and headed for the water. This time she would be the one who was early.

She placed the items in the back of the boat and went to the boathouse, where the keys were stored. Chase had given her the code for the lockbox, and she took out the squishy, floatable key chain reading "Bud's Boats." Hearing a familiar high-pitched whining sound, she located the bug spray. She didn't want mosquitoes ruining their late-night rendezvous.

Miranda doused herself with repellent. Luckily, the stuff didn't smell bad.

"Good idea," Chase said, reaching for the canister when he arrived. Then he climbed into the boat and took a seat. "Okay, this is your show. Get us out of here."

She hadn't planned this far. "Me?"

He grinned. "Yeah. Untie us and start us up."

She'd watched him, so she knew what to do. She'd

always been a fast learner. She was superaware of his scrutiny as she backed away from the dock and got the boat out onto open water.

When she exhaled a sigh of relief, Chase laughed. "You did good. Relax."

"I'm trying," Miranda replied. She headed for the closest little island, which someone had nicknamed Dill Pickle because of its shape.

"Watch the sandbar," Chase warned as she drew closer.

"I thought we'd drop anchor here. Maybe go sit on the island. I saw a campfire spot when we went by this afternoon."

"This time of year there's probably no wood," Chase said.

"That's okay. I figured we could just sit. I brought a blanket."

In the moonlight she could see Chase's lips twitch. "You and me on a blanket sounds dangerous."

"I've been thinking," she murmured. "A lot can happen in a year. You could come back married. Or not come back at all."

"Doubtful on both counts. I've already told you, I'll return in a year and take over. Here. Let me get this boat moored."

Miranda moved aside and Chase dropped anchor. "The water's about a foot deep here. We'll have to wade a little."

"That's fine." She'd worn shorts and flip-flops on purpose. They were only a few feet away from the beach.

Chase slid his shoes off and dropped them on the floor of the boat. "Where's the blanket?"

"In that bag back there."

"Got it. Let's go." He clambered out and began to wade to the island. "The rocks are a little slick, so watch out."

"I'm fine," Miranda called, lowering herself down and feeling the mossy bottom beneath her toes. She reached the shore and climbed up to the little clearing. Sand clung to her wet feet.

Chase had spread out the blanket and found the bottle of wine. He held up the cups and corkscrew in one hand, merlot in the other. "Milady?"

"It seemed like the right thing to grab at the time. I don't know. I'm improvising."

Chase sat on the blanket and opened the bottle. He handed her a cup of wine as she settled beside him. He took a drink. "So tell me, Miranda Craig, are you trying to seduce me?"

She sipped her wine. "Yes."

"You usually play life safe."

"I always will. Except for tonight." She set her cup down. "You only want me. Nothing more, right? You aren't trying to stop me from taking over?"

"No, but I will, when I return."

"In a year." She clung to that.

A year was a long time. At least that was how she rationalized her decision, to let passion rather than sensibility reign.

"For once I just want to feel. To know," she told him.

Chase set his own cup down, wedging the plastic in the sand. "So what exactly do you want from me?"

The moment of truth. Once she said the words, there would be no going back. "I want you to make love to me."

Chapter Nine

Chase coughed, trying to get his breath back. After tonight in the gazebo, he'd half expected her to retreat into her shell. Her declaration floored him.

In the moonlight she was a goddess. Her black hair shimmered. Her skin glowed like porcelain. She was the most beautiful woman he'd ever seen.

Like a siren, she planned to seduce. And he'd do anything to please her.

"I know this will be a one-night stand but only because that's all it can be. You're leaving and I just have to know what it feels like to be with you."

He reached out and stroked her cheek, his touch gentle. "Who hurt you?"

She turned her face into his palm. "Enough people. As I said, everyone's wanted something. But you don't."

"I wouldn't be so sure about that."

"No, you just want what our bodies can do together. Every kiss we've had has been magical, unlike any other. I know we'll never be together after tonight, but I wish it could be otherwise."

Her words touched him. She'd left herself open and

vulnerable, and Chase could only run his thumb along her lips. He, too, needed to know how truly being with her felt. He'd sensed something the first moment he'd met her, when she'd snapped at him because of her flat tire. He wasn't sure if his heart would survive, but tonight he would leave her well loved.

He'd spent his whole life sacrificing for the good of the cause, and this was a cause he could champion. He used his free hand to retrieve her cup and toss it aside. He wanted no regrets, no excuses.

"Make love to me," she murmured. "Show me what I've been missing. What it should feel like to be alive."

Her honesty touched him and he didn't hesitate. He could say something to reassure her, but what she wanted and needed was his lips on hers. They could talk later and he promised himself they would. He might be exiled, but he could still use the telephone. This would not be an end, but a beginning.

He found her mouth, tasted the merlot mixed with a sweetness that could only belong to her. He deepened the kiss, every one of his senses heightened by the woman in his arms. Miranda. He tried to commit every inch of her skin to memory as he slid his lips down her neck and kissed the hollow at the base of her throat.

"I've never done this before," he whispered.

"What?"

"Made love outdoors, and here. There's never been anyone else on this lake."

"Then make me the first," she begged him.

He pressed her back onto the blanket. "Yes, ma'am."

IT WAS HAPPENING. Already, her body hummed like a tightly strung bow and all Chase had done was kiss her.

She'd never felt a touch so gentle and tender. Tonight

was all about pleasure. She'd removed her bra when she'd changed, and he slid the tank top she wore off so he could bend his head and taste her taut nipple with his warm tongue. Miranda's legs clenched.

"Do you know how beautiful you are?" he asked as he bestowed the same favor to the other side.

"No," she whispered back.

"You're gorgeous." His fingers worked on her shorts. Then, as she lay naked before him, he began to drop kisses on her stomach, her exposed thighs and finally between her legs.

Miranda could do nothing but give herself over to him and the reaction he called forth from her body. She'd been right; Chase's lovemaking was unlike anything she'd experienced before. If this was just a physical connection, it was a powerful one. She'd definitely made the right decision.

"Stop thinking and relax," he told her. Then his fingers worked in tandem with his mouth and she rode both to a release that left her limp.

"Much better," he whispered. He raised himself up then, and she watched as he began to remove his shirt.

His movements were deliberate and sure, and his gaze never disconnected from hers. He dropped his shirt to ground and Miranda got her first real look at his body. He was lean and hard from exercise, and she longed to touch his honed chest and abs. She wanted to feel his arms clamped around her, skin to skin. A light breeze flitted across her heated body, but did little to cool her.

His belt went next, with a click and a slide as the buckle came undone, and a rasp as the zipper of his shorts slid down. The boxers he wore did nothing to hide his growing desire. "See what you do to me?"

"Show me…"

He smiled at her brashness.

And then he was naked, and standing before her. She reveled in how beautiful he was, and ran a finger lightly up his leg. She reached her trembling hand to stroke him.

"Am I doing this right?" she asked.

"Absolutely," he groaned.

"Then I must continue." She shifted, bringing her lips to that most intimate part of him. She only had tonight and she wanted everything. Wanted a memory burned deep, so that she'd know Mr. Right immediately, because he would be the only man who could top this moment.

Because without even entering her, Chase had already given her the best sex of her life. She wanted to please him and drive him crazy. She wanted to put all the other women he'd ever been with to shame.

"My turn," he said.

He lay down beside her. His mouth and hands roamed her body, leaving her skin tingling and sending her close to the edge again.

"Please," she gasped, and Chase obliged to fill her completely. She closed her eyes, savoring the moment.

Here she was, bathed in moonlight, with Chase deep inside her. He began to move, and she splintered, coming before he'd really begun. "That's one," he teased. "Ready for two?"

"There's more?" she panted, breathing hard as she tried to regroup.

"Much more," he promised. "In fact, you'll lose count."

"Really?"

Chase gave her another kiss. "Oh yes…"

Her "prove it" died on her lips as he changed

rhythm and brought her to somewhere her body had never been. A place where she saw stars, and not the ones in the sky above. He throbbed inside her, and she gathered him into her arms as they rode the waves together.

"Are you okay?" he whispered afterward, shifting to lie on his side facing her. He reached one arm across her body to brush the hair from her face.

"Oh no." Miranda marveled at his concern and tenderness. "I feel wonderful. That was wonderful. Thank you."

Chase's fingertips traced her eyebrows, nose and lips. They stayed like that for a long time until Miranda began to realize how exposed they were. "It's lucky you live on a very quiet lake!" she whispered.

Chase grinned. "I've been watching. No one's been by."

"They're probably all in bed."

"A great idea," he said. "But how about a swim first?"

"Swim?" She rose up on her elbows. "But I'm naked."

He chuckled. "So? I don't think the fish will mind, and the water's perfect."

A moment later, Chase was wading into the lake. "The sandbar slopes a little here, so you can get in easily and quickly." He slid into the water, and executed a short dive. When he popped up again in the moonlight, his hair and chest were gleaming. "Come on."

Miranda glanced around. They were more than a half mile from the mainland, so no one could see. Boldly, she raced into the lake, quickly wading deeper until the water covered her shoulders.

Chase was soon beside her, and he pulled her to him

and kissed her. He slipped a hand between her legs and touched her gently. "See? Lake water's good for cooling off."

As he stroked her she emitted a small cry and dropped her forehead on his shoulder.

"Ah, that's what I like," he teased.

She marveled at how sensitive she was, and how ready. "We're supposed to be cooling off."

"We have the whole night ahead of us." And with that he wrapped her legs around his waist and brought her to him. Miranda floated there as Chase made love to her again. Then they returned to shore.

"We need to go. Our bug spray's washed off and we're going to get eaten," Chase told her. "But don't think the night's done."

He tugged her tank top down over her head, and Miranda pulled on her shorts. Soon they were on their way back to the dock, Chase steering the runabout and Miranda sitting in his lap.

He docked the craft and grabbed the bag, carrying it into the boathouse to dispose of the wine and cups. Then he led Miranda to the center of the room.

His gaze searched her face. "You doing okay? No regrets?"

How could there be? This was what she wanted. Regrets could come later, once the sun came up. She knew she'd have them. But she would have regretted even more not risking, not knowing the truth of how wonderful being with Chase could be.

He bent to kiss her and she began to tug on his shirt.

"You are insatiable," he said.

"You've made me that way." She pushed him back against the pool table and pressed against him, kissing him.

"You'd better move or you're going to be in trouble. This has always been a fantasy of mine," he said when she let him come up for air.

She drew back for a moment. "You have fantasies? From the way you talked at the gazebo tonight…"

"It was all I could do not to lay you out and take you on that picnic table. That's what a pirate would do."

"Then be a pirate," she offered in a husky voice. "Claim your spoils."

"You know, I'm the one being spoiled," Chase told her after they'd made love once more. "I doubt I'll ever be able to look at this pool table again without thinking about tonight. I need to get you to bed."

For a moment she panicked. "Your grandfather. He'll know. How will I face him?"

"Shh. We'll sleep in your room. I'll leave early in the morning. He gets up after six, so we have plenty of time. Now let's go find a shower. Lake water's great, but hot water's even better."

CHASE WOKE UP at 10:00 a.m., having left Miranda about four hours earlier. He stretched, realizing his body felt great. It should; he'd had the best kind of workout a man could have.

He sobered slightly. They'd never really talked. Instead, they'd pushed everything aside and existed in a bubble of pure passion. They'd made love. He'd held her. She'd slept in his arms.

He'd had the best night of his life. For hours he'd had perfection in his grasp.

He walked to the windows and looked at the lake. Leroy stood on the end of the dock, fishing. As usual, he hadn't caught a thing.

As Chase dressed, he wondered if Miranda was

awake, and on impulse, he dialed her cell phone. She answered on the fourth ring. "Hello?"

"Hey, sleepyhead. Time to get up."

She sounded groggy and disoriented, as if she hadn't slept at all. "Who is this?"

He grinned. Poor thing was worn-out. "The guy who knows what time you got to sleep."

"Chase!" He could picture her sitting up in bed, now wide-awake.

"Hey, calm down. It's all good. My grandfather's fishing, which means he'll be on his way back to Chenille in about an hour."

"What time are we leaving?"

"Later. I still have to hoist the boat and cover it for the week. We have a cleaning service that comes every Monday, but I want to check out the boathouse and make sure we didn't leave a mess."

"Oh."

"Yeah." He heard the silence on her end. "Hey. No regrets, or I'm going to come over there and…"

He let his words drift off as she shrieked and hung up on him.

Chase left his room and went down to the dock. "Having any luck?" he asked.

"No. I just like wasting lures. I'm already packed. I was waiting for you to surface. Late night?"

"Nope," Chase lied. "I was tired, so I took advantage of being here and slept in. Getting used to the fact that after tomorrow I don't have to set my alarm clock if I don't want to."

"I haven't set mine for years." Leroy closed his tackle box. "My body wakes me at six-thirty no matter what day it is. I just gave up and got used to it. So, you good for tomorrow's board meeting? And afterward?"

"Yeah. I figured maybe I'd go to Colorado and do some mountain climbing. Brice lives out in Estes Park. You remember him?"

"Your college roommate?"

"He's some sort of park ranger at Rocky Mountain National Park. He got divorced a year ago. Figured I'd go bunk with him for a few days. Weather's perfect out there right now."

"Sounds like a good idea," Leroy said. They began to walk up to the house. "I'm glad you're making the best of this."

"It won't be so bad," Chase replied. Actually, it probably would be, but at the moment he just wanted his grandfather to leave so he could make love to Miranda again. He'd seen her in the moonlight; he wanted to see her beautiful body in daylight. As for Colorado, he hadn't even called Brice yet.

She was waiting in the great room when he and Leroy entered. "Hi," she said.

"Hey. Glad I saw you before I left," Leroy declared. "You did great this weekend. Chase will show you how to lock up. Usually I leave earlier than this, so if you sleep in you'll have to know what to do. I'll see you both tomorrow."

Fifteen minutes later, Chase and Miranda watched Leroy's Town Car drive away. Chase pulled her to him.

"Alone at last," he said.

She stiffened and he frowned. "Okay, what's wrong?"

"The night's over."

"So?" He threaded his hands into her hair and drew her face close to his. "I'm on sabbatical as of tomorrow. Let us have until then. Afterward we'll talk. See how we can make this work."

"I can't."

"Shh. You can," Chase insisted. "Let go for once."

"I let go enough last night," she said. The practical Miranda had returned. "I overslept and…"

"No regrets," he told her, releasing her. "What we had was wonderful. I'll never forget it."

"Me neither," she admitted in a voice so low he had to strain to hear. "But I'd like to get back to Chenille. I have to prepare for tomorrow, when I take over."

Disappointment consumed Chase. Then again, what had he expected? Last night had been a one-off. Two people coming together with an urgency driven by fate, passion and lust. The night was over.

She didn't want him, just his job. The one she'd have for a year. Although that was it. He didn't plan to give her one day more. Despite what had happened between them, he would never lose sight of the fact that McDaniel Manufacturing belonged to him.

"I have to put the boat away. Give me about an hour and we'll leave," Chase told her.

He began to walk away but she called to him. "Chase?"

He turned. "What?"

"Thank you for respecting my wishes."

"Yeah. No problem." He gave a curt nod and strode to the dock.

MIRANDA WATCHED CHASE from the window. She'd woken up this morning torn in half. Oh, her body thanked her. She was sore in all the right places. For one night she'd let herself loose to enjoy everything Chase offered. She loved the shower interlude, and the final lovemaking that morning before Chase headed to his room.

But the moonlight had disappeared. Tomorrow she would take over Chase's job and he would leave for parts unknown. Better to break it off now, and quickly.

That's what plain old sensible Miranda planned to do.

Besides, if she made love to Chase again she'd be doomed. Last night he'd branded her as his. If she didn't get a grip she'd pine for him the entire year.

The truth was she had work to do. One year to prove herself and make herself indispensable to the company and to Leroy. Being with Chase muddled her thoughts, made her want to throw caution to the wind. Made her think that maybe there was a way to have it all, after all.

As Chase finished with the boat and walked back toward the house, Miranda hurriedly packed. When she finished, she gave the room one final glance. This weekend would have to last her a lifetime. She wouldn't have time to date, and if she did, she already knew the results.

Chase would be impossible to top.

Chapter Ten

"So, Chase, we'll see you in a year, hey?" Nick Cissna gave him a firm handshake and a slap on the back. "You have fun. Darn, I would've loved to have the opportunity you're taking."

"Thanks," Chase said. He shook hands with a few more people as board members filed out of the conference room. It was now official. Miranda was in and Chase was on vacation, one that he'd "requested," according to the way his grandfather had presented it.

Chase watched Miranda as she spoke with Logan Bennett. He was the third most influential member of the board aside from Kathleen, the president. Logan shook Miranda's hand and the baton was passed.

Chase's tie suddenly felt tight, and he loosened the knot. No need to look perfect now. He allowed himself a wry smile. After all, he wouldn't work here for another 365 days.

"So what will you do?" Kathleen asked as she passed by.

"I'm headed to Colorado." After his stilted drive back to Chenille with Miranda, Chase had called Brice, who had been thrilled to have him come crash at his place. All Chase had to do was go by his house, put his bike on the back of his SUV and lock the doors. The vehicle was already loaded with clothes, camping gear and athletic equipment.

"Have a great time," Kathleen said.

The boardroom continued to empty and finally Miranda passed by. He touched her arm. "I'm leaving."

She bit her lip. "Okay. I'll take care of everything for you."

"I know you will. You call me, though, if you need anything. *Anything,*" he stressed, not wanting her to think he was referring to business.

"I will," she said, and sadly, he knew she wouldn't.

Chase left the boardroom and walked to his office. Time to sneak out like a thief in the night. Nothing would change in his absence. His e-mails would be forwarded to Miranda, his mail opened and distributed. Someone would come in and dust. He glanced around, his gaze alighting on the older picture of his family. On impulse, he grabbed that. Everyone was smiling, and Chase was laughing.

His throat constricted and he fought back tears. His father had always called Chase the dependable one. He wouldn't let him down now. He'd do what was asked of him.

He pocketed the picture. Then he took a deep breath and turned out the light. The mountains waited.

BY THE MIDDLE OF JULY, Chase had climbed nearly every peak in Rocky Mountain National Park. He'd just completed his final challenge. He stood atop Longs Peak, over 14,000 feet above sea level, and inhaled the thin air.

He'd been away from Chenille for six weeks. He'd

crashed on Brice's couch for a week, and then, with a bit of good fortune, had managed to find lodging at the YMCA camp outside Estes Park. The Y had some of the best recreational programs and facilities around, and guests could even hike into Rocky Mountain National Park from the grounds. Preferring the laid-back atmosphere to a hotel, he'd been in his one-bedroom cabin ever since. It was his base of operations as he made day trips up through the alpine meadows and longer excursions into Wyoming for white-water rafting.

"Wow! This is great!"

"Yeah," Chase replied, taking a drink of water. He was on an organized hike, and he'd partnered with Rachel, an enthusiastic college student he'd met. She was working at the camp and would return to Colorado State in the fall.

She was pretty and loved all things outdoors, but she was thirteen years his junior and couldn't compare to Miranda.

No one he'd met had.

He opened his backpack and withdrew his digital 35mm SLR camera. He'd added photography to his list of hobbies and even purchased a few lenses. Tomorrow he'd leave here and take Interstate 70 east. He planned on making day stops in Kansas City, Saint Louis and Indianapolis before ending up in New York just in time to become an uncle.

He'd heard Cecilia was having a girl.

He lifted the camera and started taking pictures. He could see as far as Wyoming.

"Let me get one of both of you," someone said, and he threw his arm around Rachel's shoulders and obliged.

"You have to e-mail me a copy," she told him, and

Chase agreed. Then there was an obligatory group shot, a moment preserved in history of a bunch of people who had climbed a mountain together, yet wouldn't keep in touch after today.

The guide called time, and began gathering the hikers together. They'd started at 3:00 a.m., and if they left the summit now they could beat the dangerous afternoon storms that often developed. Chase gazed across at the Twin Sisters peaks, took a picture and put his camera away.

Rachel kept up both her pace and her chatter the entire descent. "So you're leaving when?" she asked a mile before they reached the trailhead.

"Tomorrow," Chase replied.

"A bunch of my friends and I are hitting Eddie's tonight. You should come with us. Don't say you're too tired, or that you have to pack. You should party on your last night. Hey, you've got to celebrate. We conquered Longs."

While he wasn't interested in Rachel romantically, the idea of hanging out with people sounded appealing. He could have all his stuff loaded into the SUV within an hour. "Tonight could work."

"Oh, you'll have fun, especially if you like darts," Rachel said.

Chase half listened to her next story. His mind was on the last part of the hike, and contemplating the week ahead. His real contact with his family had been through e-mails or text messages.

Chandy had taken off with friends to California. Chris and his wife were selling their house and buying another. Cecilia declared she was huge and couldn't wait to see him. He missed her, too. Of all his siblings, she'd always been the closest.

He'd spoken to his grandfather a few times, but Leroy had never been one to spend hours on the phone. He'd been brief, said he felt great and that Miranda was doing a great job.

Chase wanted to know more, but even when he'd asked, Leroy had told him not to worry, and failed to elaborate. So Chase had no idea what was happening at McDaniel. Or if Miranda had met anyone new.

He was in the dark.

"Sorry, I missed that," Chase said, realizing Rachel had asked him a question. She repeated it, and he focused, trying to stay in the present and on the trail.

When they reached the parking lot, he unlocked his vehicle and removed his cell phone. Not wanting to be distracted during the climb, he'd left it in the car.

He flipped open the phone. "Let me have your number," he told Rachel. "I'll call you later and get directions."

"Great."

Chase began to hit the directory, but his phone beeped as it registered voice mail. "Hold on. Let me check if this is Brice. He might want to go."

"The more the merrier," she replied.

Chase had three messages. He hadn't had that many in one day since he'd left Chenille. The first was from Miranda, sent around 10:00 a.m. She'd asked him to call back as soon as possible.

Chase frowned. Why would she be phoning him after six weeks? He gripped the phone tighter. She'd said she was on the pill. But what if she was pregnant? His mind raced and he almost didn't hear the start of the second message, which was indeed from Brice. He wanted to get together for a beer before Chase left.

The last message had been sent only a half hour ago.

He recognized Cecilia's voice, but he could hardly make out what his sister was saying, since she was sobbing so hard. He heard her gasp out "hospital" and he panicked, wondering if she'd lost the baby. Surely she was too far along for that.

"Call me, Chase, the moment you get this. I'm on my way to the airport. I know I'm not supposed to fly, but this is an emergency." She'd calmed down and focused. "I just have to be there. He could die. Chase, call me. Hurry."

Chase could sense Rachel's query. He held up a finger and hit a button on his speed dial.

His sister answered on the first ring. "Thank God it's you," she said.

"What's going on?"

He heard her sniffle. "Grandpa had a heart attack. He's in the hospital in the Twin Cities. I've been in touch, but you're the power of attorney and his health care director."

Chase remembered the papers he'd signed, giving him permission to carry out Leroy's wishes not to resuscitate. He felt weak-kneed and sick. "Are we at that point?"

"I don't think so. I hope not. He can't die, Chase. What will we do?"

His decision was instantaneous. This was when Chase was at his best. Brice, Rachel and Eddie's would have to wait. He would see his family through this crisis. "I'm on my way."

MIRANDA PACED the waiting room. She'd been there since late Saturday afternoon, arriving a few hours after Leroy had been airlifted from the hospital closest to Lone Pine. The E.R. doctors at the first hospital had diagnosed him with heart failure. They'd stabilized him, but the best place for surgery would be in Minneapolis–Saint Paul, so they'd sent him to a hospital in the Twin Cities. Her newly purchased GPS unit had come in handy as she'd made the drive in her car.

She poured another cup of coffee. She'd lost track of time and how many cups she'd had in her attempt to stay awake.

The wall clock read 7:00 a.m. It was Sunday morning.

She'd learned Leroy had made it through surgery, but that was all she knew.

Chase hadn't called, but Cecilia was on her way. She'd texted a message before boarding, to say her flight would land at nine.

Miranda sank onto the seat. Never in a million years had she expected this. She'd driven to the lake Friday evening, and she and Leroy had eaten dinner. He'd been chipper and upbeat when she'd met with him in the morning to discuss business. After lunch, he'd told her he was off for his daily siesta.

For the past few weeks she'd been leaving around noon. But yesterday the water had called to her. Not confident in the motorboat without Chase, she'd taken out a canoe. She'd paddled for hours, until her arms ached.

She missed Chase. Sleeping above the kitchen kept alive the night they'd shared there. She hadn't heard from him, and Leroy hadn't ventured any details. She'd reached for the phone several times since he'd been gone, and then she'd set it aside. They had to walk these separate paths. It was better this way.

Miranda bit back tears. She'd lost Chase. She couldn't lose Leroy, too. It had been close. The paramedics had told her that if she hadn't stayed those extra hours Leroy wouldn't have had a chance. He'd had a heart attack in his sleep. She'd gone to check on him when he wasn't in the great room on her return from canoeing, and found him lying in bed, looking far too pale and still. When he hadn't responded to her attempts to wake him, she'd called 911.

Miranda dropped her head in her hands. She'd gotten only an hour of sleep here and there and she was exhausted. The staff said they'd come and get her if something changed. She wondered if they'd forgotten her.

"Leroy McDaniel's room."

She started, turning her head so sharply she almost wrenched her neck. She knew that voice.

"Chase." She rose to her feet. "You're here."

He turned, his eyes raking over her. She knew what he saw: a woman wearing yesterday's shorts and T-shirt. She hadn't even washed her face or put on makeup.

"Yeah." He tapped his fingers on the counter as the floor nurse did something with her computer.

"They won't tell me anything," Miranda said. He was such a sight for sore eyes! Unlike her, in her rumpled clothing, he wore pressed pants and a short-sleeve polo.

"They will me." Chase handed over a document. "This is his living will and health care directive. I have a legal right to all information. I'm Chase McDaniel. I'm also his next of kin."

The woman looked over at the document. "Yes, Mr. McDaniel. If you'll take a seat we'll get this processed and have someone with you in just a moment."

Chase nodded before walking toward Miranda. "You look like hell. Haven't you slept?"

She ignored his rough, worried tone. "How could I?"

"I'm here now. I'll handle everything." He reached

into his pocket and pulled out a hotel key. "I got a room at…" He named a nearby premier hotel. "Room 315. Go get some sleep and I'll call you in a little while. My sister's got the adjoining room, so the interior door might be open. At least that's what the reception people told me. I had someone meet me at the airport. I chartered a small plane and flew in."

His efficiency, plus his ability to climb on a small plane when one had killed his parents, stunned Miranda. "What about your car?"

"I hired a service to drive it home."

She stared at him. He had taken over like a man adept at handling any crisis. Chase didn't think of himself. He figured out what needed to be done and he did it. "Okay."

"Go," he ordered, his tone gently insistent.

Miranda felt the weight of the world leave her. Chase was here. He would handle everything. It would all be okay.

BY SUNDAY AFTERNOON all of Chase's siblings had arrived. Leroy had undergone bypass surgery Saturday night and was still in intensive care. Now rested and showered, Miranda returned to the hospital.

"He's sleeping," Chase told her when she asked. "Thank you for being there for him."

"I'm so glad I was," Miranda replied. "So what can I do?"

Chase ran a hand through his hair. He'd let it grow out, and he needed both a shave and a cut. "Seriously? Go back to Chenille."

That was not the answer she'd been expecting. She bristled. "Excuse me?"

"By tomorrow McDaniel Manufacturing will be inundated with phone calls. Your presence will keep everyone calm. You need to do that until I arrive and take over."

The businessman was in full force. She registered his last words: *take over.* "Which is when?" she asked.

"I'm probably not going to get down there for a few more days. I have to make sure Leroy pulls through first. Then he'll have to recuperate somewhere, which means a home nurse back in Chenille. There's no way he can stay at the lake in this condition. I'll get my grandfather settled and then I'll come straighten out McDaniel."

"McDaniel is doing fine." Miranda crossed her arms and stood her ground.

"Never said it wasn't. But I'm back now and this is my company. The line of succession has always been clear." He gave her a tight smile.

"Chase?" Cecilia had entered the waiting room. "The doctor wants to meet with us."

"Okay. Give me a second." Chase faced Miranda, determination etching the lines of his face. "I'll call you later today. You need to have Sarah in PR issue a press release. The only reason this has been kept quiet so far is because his heart attack happened at the lake. Communities like Chenille tend to get nervous, especially since we're the biggest employer in town. I'll give you the details Sarah needs when I call. Also, there's an emergency plan. It should be in a binder in my office. Have Carla give it to you."

"I'll call Sarah when I get back," Miranda said, knowing now was not the time to confront Chase about his taking over.

"Do that," he replied. And then he turned and left the room.

MIRANDA WATCHED CHASE GO. While she hadn't expected him to run into her arms, she'd at least hoped for a hug after not seeing him for six weeks.

But Chase had seemed almost like a machine. Focused. Deliberate. Adept in a crisis, but not very warm or reachable.

She decided to give him some leeway. He'd almost lost his grandfather. That was devastating enough to make anyone turn off his emotions.

She walked out to the car and prepared for the drive back to Chenille. She would run everything in Leroy's absence, which was what she'd been prepared to do. It was a challenge she was ready for.

She picked up the phone and made a call. She'd spoken to Walter once already and told him she'd keep him informed. "Hi. No, no, Leroy's pulled through the night. It's looking good. I just thought you should know Chase is back."

IT WAS THURSDAY, almost two full weeks following Leroy's surgery, when Chase walked into the headquarters of McDaniel Manufacturing.

His grandfather was in stable condition and had returned to Chenille yesterday. The doctors were optimistic that Leroy would have a complete recovery—if nothing caused him any stress.

Chase hit the button for the executive floor. All four grandchildren had agreed that Leroy shouldn't have anything to do with work for the next six weeks. They'd also insisted that he have a live-in, round-the-clock nurse. That was the number one thing on Chase's agenda today.

Number two was dealing with a very annoying Walter Peters, who had sent Chase an e-mail suggesting he leave the company in Miranda's capable hands and continue his sabbatical as Leroy wanted.

As if. Chase wondered if Miranda was behind Walter's correspondence. She hadn't been too happy with some of the directives he'd given her this past week.

Chase left the elevator and approached Leroy's office. Ethel, his grandfather's secretary, jumped to her feet.

"How is he?" she asked.

"Back home in Chenille as of yesterday," he replied.

"Oh thank God." Ethel sank back into her chair. "I've been so worried. Everyone has."

"He's getting better every day. The surgery went well. He's going to be fine."

Tears formed in Ethel's eyes. "I'm so glad." She'd been Leroy's secretary for more than thirty years, and was practically a member of the family.

"Me, too," Chase told her. He filled her in on what the doctors said. "So Leroy sleeps a lot, but that's normal. We have to hire a nurse. The one who traveled with him can only stay another day or two."

Ethel dabbed at her eyes with a tissue. "Do you want me to find one?"

"That would be wonderful."

"I'd be more than happy to. My sister had to have a nurse a few years ago. We were very pleased with the company we used. I'll get right on it. I need something to do. Ms. Craig had pretty much taken over even before Leroy's heart attack. Now with him gone, I'm really getting antsy."

Chase understood how she felt. "Well, that's about to change. I have Carla, but I'm also going to need your help. I'm back and I'm taking over."

Ethel's eyes widened. "But Ms. Craig…"

"Has been filling my shoes while I'm gone. She was not hired to do my grandfather's job. I'm next in line. This is my family company."

"Of course it is." Ethel covered her reaction quickly, but Chase still saw her surprise. Miranda must have told everyone otherwise, for Ethel asked the question that probably all his employees wondered. "But what about your vacation?"

"My year-long absence has been cut short. My grandfather won't be back for a while, and McDaniel Manufacturing needs a McDaniel at the helm. That's my role."

"I know you'll do a fine job."

The vote of confidence was what Chase needed, especially since Walter was a wild card. Chase wouldn't be surprised if he tried to have the board place his protégée at the helm instead of him.

As for Miranda, despite what they'd shared, Chase couldn't discount her ambitions. While he hoped she wouldn't be cutthroat, with Leroy out of commission and Walter making waves, Chase knew he had to watch his back.

"Ethel, I'll need you to alert the board of the change in leadership. I also need you to get me copies of everything that's crossed Leroy's desk since I've been gone. I'm out of the loop and I needed to catch up yesterday."

"Absolutely. Anything you need." Ethel would get right on it. She was tops, and her loyalty lay with the McDaniel family.

"We'll let my grandfather's office sit empty until we know when he's coming back."

"Will he be back?" Ethel asked.

Chase's lips thinned into a tight line. Leroy would

not return if his grandchildren had their way. "I don't know. So leave his office and don't let anyone in there. Forward everything he deals with to me."

"It's good to have you back, Chase."

"Thanks, Ethel." He gave her a smile and headed for his office, which was around the corner from his grandfather's.

He'd told Carla he was coming, yet she rose to her feet when he approached. "Chase!"

He was glad to see her and gave her a quick hug. "Hey. Ready to get to work?"

Carla nodded. "Absolutely. I knitted an entire afghan for your sister's baby while you were gone. Ms. Craig's secretary hasn't needed a thing. You can only play so much solitaire, and my credit card can't take much more online shopping."

"Well, get ready to put your nose to the grindstone." He repeated what he'd told Ethel. "Both of you will work together to help me."

"Of course. Whatever you need."

"What I need is to see Ms. Craig. Will you call her and request she meet me here in thirty minutes?" With that Chase entered his office and flipped on the light. Everything looked exactly as he'd left it. He reached into his briefcase and returned the family portrait to its spot. He also found a place for the new digital picture frame he'd bought at the hospital gift shop. He'd already uploaded the device with his Colorado pictures and shared them with Leroy while he recuperated at the hospital.

He sat behind his desk, taking a moment to absorb the feeling. For the six weeks before Leroy's heart attack Chase had had no agenda. He'd been hanging out in one of the most beautiful parts of the United States. While the mountains had been majestic and awe-inspiring, they didn't evoke the satisfaction coursing through him right now. This was what fit him best. This office was where he belonged.

He was home.

MIRANDA FUMED as she got ready to meet with Chase.

He was back.

Worse, he was staying. Walter had said he'd told him to go, but so far Chase hadn't. Nor did it appear as if he intended to.

Miranda picked up a mechanical pencil and tapped the eraser end on her desk. The motion did little to release her frustration, or to reduce the migraine starting behind her left eyebrow.

She should be thrilled to see him. She'd missed him. Sort of. In fact, she'd kept herself so busy she hadn't had time to worry about "that night" and what it meant. She'd immersed herself in work.

She'd pretty much been running the company, as Leroy, on his summer schedule, had turned over many of his day-to-day responsibilities. She was doing Chase's job and more.

Now she'd been ordered to Chase's office like a student called to the principal. She fingered the two-inch binder labeled McDaniel Emergency Plan. The company had detailed instructions outlining procedures for everything from earthquakes to tornadoes. McDaniel Manufacturing even had a terrorist plan.

They'd prepared for everything except succession; the directions were woefully inadequate for that particular circumstance. Walter had told Miranda that he was working on the board, feeling them out. He'd assured her that Chase wouldn't fire her, which was Miranda's worst-case scenario.

Her phone rang, making her jump. She took a deep breath to calm herself, and reached for the receiver. "Miranda Craig."

"I didn't want you to be late," her secretary said.

"Thanks," Miranda replied, replacing the handset. She stood and tried to smooth out the wrinkles in her skirt. Time to face Chase.

CHASE ROSE TO HIS FEET when Miranda entered the room. As it had that first day he'd seen her, his throat constricted and his temperature soared. He stepped out from behind his desk to greet her, as he would any other colleague.

Except Miranda wasn't any other colleague. He'd made love to her, multiple times. She'd given him the best night of his life.

Instead, as he said, "Miranda," and guided her to the chair in front of his desk, he knew that that one night was all he'd ever have with her. No matter how much his body wanted her, his mind had to focus on what was important, especially when Walter was trying to unseat him. Chase knew he had to choose: Miranda or McDaniel Manufacturing. He wasn't the type to delude himself into believing he could have both, not at this critical juncture.

While Leroy had promised Chase he would be CEO, the terms of the deal were known only to the two of them, Miranda and Walter. The board would not necessarily honor an agreement they had known nothing about. They could easily unseat Chase if Walter got his way.

Chase refused to let that happen.

Miranda would probably hate him before the week was out. He understood her well enough to know she wasn't going to like him taking away her power.

He sank into his big leather chair wishing things

could be different between them. "Thank you for meeting with me."

"I didn't think I could ignore your summons. However, I'm not a child needing to be called into the principal's office, and I'd like you to treat me better."

His eyes narrowed at her description. She didn't plan to hold anything back. She wasn't happy with his return. Well, he'd always warned her today would come. It had just arrived earlier than expected. "I'm sorry if you felt that way."

She leaned forward and her white shirt gaped a little, showing him a hint of smooth skin where he'd placed hungry kisses. He'd tasted her, and could remember all the little cries she'd made. He knew that there could be no more. Yet she sat across from him, a siren that lured. Why had he thought making love to Miranda would get her out of his system? This was torture.

"What else would I think, Chase? In the past you've hovered in my doorway whenever you needed to talk to me. I recognize a power play when I see one. Well, I'm here, so let's get this started. I don't have time to waste. I have a lunch meeting with the president of the Chamber of Commerce at noon."

Chase focused on her face. Damn, she was beautiful, even when she was angry. He couldn't help staring at her lips, thinking about the way her mouth had moved over his skin. He tried to concentrate on delivering the news. He couldn't afford to get distracted.

"I wanted you to know I've spoken with most of the board members by conference call. I'm taking over my grandfather's position. We'll hold an emergency meeting this upcoming Monday afternoon to formalize the arrangement naming me CEO. The only opposition seems to be from Walter."

A little V formed between her eyebrows. "I thought Leroy was doing better."

"He'll need at least six weeks for physical therapy. He's not to have anything stress him, including work. Not even one hint of office drama is to reach his ears. I've started reviewing everything that's been done in my absence. I expect to be at full speed tomorrow. I don't want anything to interrupt this transition, including Walter. Or you." There. Chase didn't like being so harsh, but he had to make things clear.

She sat back and folded her hands in her lap, the earlier fight gone. The view of skin vanished and he found himself disappointed on both counts. "So I report to you."

"Yes." The feeling of victory should have been sweet as he said the word, but oddly it wasn't. He cared about his competitor. That had never happened before.

"And the board will approve this," she pressed. Chase's eyes narrowed.

"They will Monday. I've reached enough of them to secure a majority. It's not worth you or Walter attempting a coup."

She sat there so primly that he wished for the earlier spitfire to return. "So you'll override your grandfather's wish for you to remain away for a year."

"Since the board doesn't know about that, it's not an issue. Besides, Leroy didn't foresee this situation. And what kind of a grandson would I be if I didn't return to ensure the success of my family firm? Given the circumstances, I really don't think I need to be out jaunting around the country. I'm Leroy's power of attorney. I vote his stock and I sign his bills if he's incapacitated. The entire family is in agreement. None of us want to lose him, or our company. A McDaniel has always been CEO and that's the way things are going to stay."

"I see. Well then. If there's nothing else?" Miranda stood.

Still seated, Chase studied her. He'd loved every inch of her body and now there was a rift the size of the Grand Canyon between them. He hated it. Even sparring was better than the chill setting over them. "We're finished here. You can go."

"Thank you." Miranda walked out, and Chase released the pent-up breath he hadn't realized he'd been holding.

He wanted to follow her to her office, shut the door, sweep everything off her desk like in a movie, and make love to her until both of them were sated and the chasm between them had disappeared. Only in bed had there been no walls, no pretense. Only then had they been themselves, without agendas.

But McDaniel Manufacturing came first. He had to remember it was nothing personal, just business. Chase reached for a report.

THANKFULLY, Miranda's knees didn't wobble until she reached her office. Then she trembled all the way to the safety of her desk chair. There was no way she could work like this.

She'd made a grave tactical error in making love with Chase. She'd assumed she had a year before seeing him again. She'd figured by then they'd have moved on.

Instead, she had an immediate physical response to him that had left her shaking. She had far too many graphic memories of their time together. Although, obviously that night didn't mean much to him.

The proof had been behind his desk, on the digital picture frame. When the photo of him with his arm around some girl appeared, Miranda had felt her heart fall to her feet. It sure hadn't taken long to be replaced.

To him, their weekend had been casual sex between two people who were intensely attracted to each other. Sex didn't equal to love, so why did it bother her so much that he'd moved on?

Her cell phone rang, jarring her from her depressing line of thought. She dug the device out of her purse and answered. "Miranda Craig."

"Thought you might need a friend."

Walter. "You've obviously heard."

"I received a call from Ethel about ten minutes ago, asking me to attend a board meeting."

"He's taking over for his grandfather. He told me he has majority support."

"And he might," Walter replied. "What about you? Can you handle this arrangement? You'd still be second in command."

"I'm going to have to try."

"Why?" Walter asked. "Leroy had no intention for Chase to come back before a year was up. I've already told Chase that. He knows I oppose his return. Leroy wanted him to have this time off."

"Yes, but circumstances change," Miranda replied.

"Miranda, you were born for this job. It's what your parents would've wanted for you. Don't let a bad situation scare you away."

"Chase is family." She swiveled so she could look out the window. Everything she could see was part of McDaniel Manufacturing. This was Chase's birthright. Why had she deluded herself it could be otherwise?

Walter didn't buy that argument. "Chase is also a playboy who has had everything handed to him. He's lacked direction. He's been spoiled."

"He seems adept at crisis management." Miranda defended Chase despite herself. Within minutes of his arrival at the hospital, the doctors had given Chase full details on Leroy's condition. Miranda hadn't been able to get squat.

"Miranda, you have a contract with McDaniel. You're not going to lose your job. I've assured you of that. But what do you want?"

Chase.

Now where had that thought come from? "I was supposed to have at least a year to learn the ropes. I don't have the experience to run this firm."

"Neither do half the other guys who become CEOs. They learn as they go. Some of the best ones I've seen have been upstarts. They have fresh ideas. Unless you tell me otherwise, I'm going to make a motion that Chase stand down, as Leroy requested, until his year is up."

Miranda closed her eyes as her growing migraine sent lancing pain through her head. Some black clouds had lifted. But with Walter's offer others had blown in to take their place. "Thank you for your support, but do you mind if I think about this first?"

"Think hard. Unless you tell me not to, I'm going to make a motion to unseat Chase. And Miranda, even though Chase is a McDaniel, I'm Leroy's best friend. I have just as much sway with these people as Chase does. I've been meeting with them for twenty years. If I reveal the truth about Leroy's wishes, they'll change their minds and the job will be yours."

After promising to call Walter before Monday, Miranda set her phone down. She stared around her office. She'd signed a contract when she'd taken the McDaniel job. She'd be committing career suicide if she resigned this quickly. She could probably contact a headhunter and have him or her start quietly making inquiries, but Chenille had grown on her. Miranda had fallen in love with the little town. She'd begun to build a life here.

Her younger sister had even come by three weeks ago and commented on how content Miranda appeared. And she had been, until Leroy's heart attack and Chase's return.

Walter had just handed her her dream back. If anyone could convince the board to give Miranda the CEO job, it was him.

But the giddy feeling that she'd gotten months ago upon being hired didn't come. Instead, doom and gloom stole over her. This was corporate politics. She was running with the big dogs; she had to play hardball.

Yet, deep down, Miranda was a person who cared. It shouldn't matter that Chase would hate her for the rest of her days if Walter's motion overturned his, but it did. And he'd moved on.

She had to toughen up.

Chapter Eleven

Mike Storm had lived in Chenille his whole life. A friendly looking man in his mid-forties, he owned the local furniture store. He was also the Chamber of Commerce president, a member of the Lions Club and the secretary of the school board.

He hadn't come to lunch alone, Miranda noted as she followed Diane to a table in one of Maxine's back rooms. Mike saw her approach and stood. So did the man who had his back to her.

The interloper didn't even need to turn around. Miranda already recognized him.

Chase had crashed her lunch.

"Miranda." Mike reached out and grasped her hand in his bruising grip. "I'm so glad you and Chase agreed to meet with me."

"The chamber is very important us," she managed to answer as she extracted her hand. At least the pain kept her from wanting to reach over and punch Chase in the nose. How dare he! This was her meeting.

"I was just telling Chase that we've gotten a nibble. Rhodes Printing is expanding. They're looking to build a new plant in the Midwest and Chenille's made their short list of potential locations."

"That's great news," Miranda replied, taking the seat next to Mike's, which put her directly across from Chase. "When will the final decision be made?"

"They're sending a scouting party here in two weeks and they'll stay five days while Iowa and Chenille woo them with our proposal. I've already contacted the governor's office and the state development agency, and I'll be meeting with them tomorrow so we can get our presentation together. Three hundred permanent jobs based right here."

"I'm sure you'll do a fantastic sales job." Miranda said.

Mike reached for his iced tea. "Thanks, but we'll need McDaniel's help."

"Anything we can do." Chase jumped into the conversation as their waitress brought Miranda some iced tea. At Maxine's, once you were a regular, the staff knew what you wanted and brought it without being asked.

"We've never had this type of interest in our town. When I requested this meeting it was to ask McDaniel to underwrite a fall festival we'd like to hold in October. But Rhodes Printing's expansion is much more important."

"I agree," Chase said.

Mike had clearly given the matter some thought. "We need slick brochures on why Chenille is a great place to live, raise a family and locate your company. Who better to answer those questions than McDaniel employees?"

"So we'd be a two-horse town." Chase laughed. "We contract all our four-color press printing and binding with a plant in Kansas City. I'd be more than happy to transfer our business to Rhodes Printing provided they give us a comparable bid."

Chase named the figure they'd spent last year on annual reports and other company brochures. "We're a pretty large account and lately I haven't been that satisfied. It seems sort of like we're being taken for granted, as if we'll always be a client. Rhodes could definitely win our business."

"I appreciate your willingness to help," Mike said. "Chenille is McDaniel's town."

"We can be good neighbors," Chase replied. "I'd be happy to meet with representatives of their company if that will do some good. We've kept all our manufacturing here for a reason, instead of having multiple plants across the country. What tax abatements do they want?"

Miranda listened as Chase and Mike talked tax incentives. While the conversation went on without her, she found the entire discussion fascinating. She'd watched Walter and Leroy conduct business, but since they'd only had a week's transition, she'd never seen Chase interact with anyone outside of McDaniel.

He'd known the amount of their printing costs off the top of his head. He could remember business expenses from the last plant expansion, five years ago.

He also understood the ramifications of three hundred new jobs. While not all the employees would live in Chenille, enough would that the school system would have an influx of new families, which might make for overcrowding.

What was supposed to be an hour lunch for the fall festival became a brainstorming session for the best way to entice Rhodes Printing without sacrificing Chenille and Iowa values.

Considering Miranda hadn't lived in Chenille or Iowa that long, she had little to add. Which might be exactly what Chase was trying to prove, she realized as lunch wound down.

On one hand, he was showing her how competent he really was. The guy knew his stuff. He was sharp and savvy. He didn't just spout figures, he lived them. Chenille and McDaniel Manufacturing were in his blood.

The flip side was that his expertise made her appear incompetent. He'd taken over her meeting without any effort at all. What he'd done had been designed to prove she was in over her head and not as qualified as he was for Leroy's job.

In fact, as the waitress came by and offered coffee and dessert, Chase committed several thousand dollars to get the fall festival off the ground. He didn't even ask to see the proposal, just gave Mike his word that McDaniel would help out financially, and stated his maximum monetary figure.

"You've been more than generous," Mike said, obviously moved as Chase even brushed off his offer to pick up the tab for lunch. "Thank you."

"As you say, McDaniel and Chenille are synonymous. We love this town. Anything you can do at the chamber to provide a better quality of life for our employees and local residents is worth supporting."

Mike glanced at his watch. "I've got to get going. I've got a conference call with the governor's office in an hour."

"Don't let us keep you. Miranda and I are fine finishing dessert on our own."

"Thanks again, Chase. Miranda." With that, he left.

Miranda looked at her barely touched slice of strawberry-covered pound cake. Mike had polished off his dessert in record time. Chase was halfway through his apple pie.

The room had emptied and they were the last diners seated, although a few people remained in another section, visible through an archway. She should make her excuses, get up and leave.

"You've been quiet all day." As if sensing her impending flight, Chase broke the ice before she could set her napkin on the table.

She shrugged. "You pretty much took over and said everything. I didn't really have anything to add."

"Hmm." Chase's lips wrapped around the tines of his fork as he ate another morsel. The man could make eating dessert sexy. "Your being speechless is not normal."

She rose to the bait. "You showing up uninvited at my lunch is rude."

He chuckled, clearly enjoying her reaction. "There's the spitfire. I knew she couldn't have died. Actually, I did get invited."

The man was infuriating. "Then it was rude not to tell me."

He shrugged and took another bite. "How could I? You were already here."

"Okay, you'd better explain. This is making no sense." He'd already made her feel incompetent. She refused to feel stupid, as well, no matter how his smile warmed her insides.

"I came in for lunch. Mike saw me and invited me to join him, as he'd just heard this great news. End of story."

"You knew I was coming here. You could have eaten elsewhere."

"Where? This is Chenille."

True. Everyone ate at Maxine's. "It was *my* meeting."

"Things change. And we gave him the money he wanted. He's happy and he probably won't spend close to that much. Mike's great at making money stretch."

"You don't even know if McDaniel can afford what you offered."

"Sure we can. I read the quarterly reports yesterday. We're actually twelve percent ahead of our net profit projections for the year. We have room to put our focus on what's important."

"You didn't even look at his proposal first to see what he wants to do."

Chase's shoulders lifted. "So? I don't need to. I know Mike. Have for years. He doesn't do anything half-assed. If he's going to put on a fall festival, it'll be one heck of a good time. And October is perfect because he can tie it into the high school's homecoming game. This town loves a party, and people will come from miles around. This could become an annual tradition, drawing tons of tourists."

"You didn't consult me on what I thought."

"I don't have to."

The authoritative way he said it had the hairs of her neck standing on end. "The meeting was mine. I was to review the proposal. You cannot just come in here and do whatever you want."

Her rebuke was sharp, yet Chase's words were even sharper. "Yes, I can."

Miranda leaned back as if slapped. She took a moment to compose herself, controlling the fury that threatened to make her leap out of the chair and throttle him. This was why this arrangement of Chase filling in for Leroy wasn't going to work.

"Chase, whether you like it or not, I am McDaniel's vice president. You might be taking over for your grandfather, but that doesn't mean you can delegate me into oblivion. I have a job to do and I plan to do it."

"And I never said you wouldn't. You're taking something personally that you shouldn't. This is business."

"No, this is childish. I am competent enough to do my job, which included dealing with the fall festival."

"Fine. You can oversee the money and have Mike report to you. In a few days I'll have a firm grip on everything and I'll also have your role clearly defined. Until then, I'm sorry if things aren't quite to your satisfaction. There's a lot of data to sort through from the past seven weeks."

"You could have just asked me to brief you instead of acting like some gorilla pounding his chest."

His gaze narrowed. "I like to do things my way."

"Yeah, that's obvious." She pushed her plate away, her appetite gone. "Fine, by Monday afternoon following the board meeting I'll expect you to have my role defined and my duties outlined. I find having my time wasted insulting."

"So take the rest of today and tomorrow off with pay. Have a mini vacation on me. Enjoy yourself."

She gaped at him. He was essentially banishing her, as his grandfather had him. "You are a grade A jerk."

Chase didn't appear to be insulted. "Didn't you once say you'd be grateful to be in my shoes? Here's your chance. Go to a spa or something. Drive to the Twin Cities and shop."

He knew she'd do neither. Miranda stood, towering over him. She'd always considered herself a calm, rational person, but at the moment she would have liked to take the remains of her iced tea and dump it over Chase's head. "Thank you for lunch," she said as she strode away.

"Everything okay, Ms. Craig?" Diane asked as she stalked past her.

She plastered a smile on her face. "Everything was wonderful," she lied.

Bright sunlight assaulted her as she left the restaurant. The July day was ninety-nine degrees but even the summer heat couldn't warm the chill that had gripped Miranda's heart.

CHASE PAID THE BILL and tucked the receipt away.

He'd done it again. He'd been a complete ass to Miranda. What was it about her that rubbed him the wrong way?

Actually, when they'd been together, nothing had. Everything had been so right. That was the problem.

He wrestled with his feelings as he walked to his car. He was angry that Walter planned to try to unseat him. Chase was resentful that Miranda couldn't be happy as a vice president, an impressive position in itself.

However, he'd acted like a jerk and he had no rational explanation for his behavior. Miranda had been doing a fine job in his absence. Maybe he was jealous he'd been replaced so easily. Was that why he'd acted as he had?

Or was it because he'd secretly hoped that when he returned she'd fall into his arms instead of looking straight through him as if nothing had happened between them?

Whatever his reasons, he'd behaved like a dog marking its territory. Absolutely abominable. He owed her yet another apology.

But when Chase returned to work, he learned that she'd taken his advice. She'd left for the day and told her secretary she'd be back Monday morning.

"You can reach her on her cell phone if it's anything important," her secretary offered. "Do you need the number?"

"No, I've got it." Chase headed to his office and closed the door. He checked his e-mails and read something that bothered him a great deal.

No wonder Miranda had hightailed it out of Dodge.

To hell with apologizing. Why should he feel guilty? One of McDaniel's board meeting rules was that no new business could be brought to the board without being placed on the agenda first.

There, in black type, was proof that Walter planned to make a motion to unseat Chase and put Miranda in his place.

Chase fumed. He had no problem with her being vice president, but she wasn't going to be CEO.

If she wanted that, it would be over his dead body.

Chapter Twelve

Upon leaving McDaniel for the day, Miranda had gone back to her apartment and sulked. Then she'd grabbed a pen and paper and made a list of all the reasons why she should hate Chase McDaniel. Eventually she'd calmed down and made a list of all the reasons why she'd be a great CEO.

She didn't get very far on the second list, so she set it aside. She knew by Monday she needed to be prepared. Walter might make the argument for her, but if the board, or even Chase, pinned her for specifics, she had to be ready. The board meeting would be like a job interview from hell, times one hundred.

Chase had told her to go to a spa, for goodness' sake. Her ire again bubbling, Miranda kicked off her shoes and glanced at her toes. Okay, she could use a pedicure. But that didn't make him right.

She looked around her apartment. On the table were flyers from the real estate agent advertising about half a dozen houses for her to look at this weekend. House hunting would have to be postponed.

Sitting in this apartment would also have to wait. If

she stayed another minute she'd go berserk. Miranda went to her bedroom and changed clothes.

She knew what she needed to do.

AFTER SPENDING THE afternoon trying to work, Chase gave up. His concentration was shot. He was still mad about the fight ahead. And he couldn't get Miranda off his mind. He should hate her. Oddly, he didn't. For the past ten minutes he'd instead been thinking about that first time on the island. There had been purity in their actions. No agendas. No secrets. Just two souls finding each other.

Okay, he needed a break. He needed to get out and run or bike, but the temperature outside had cracked triple digits—100 degrees.

He'd have to swim. He could do at least an hour's worth of laps in his grandfather's pool. He'd bring the work on his desk home and finish it tonight, after he'd exhausted himself. It was only an hour or so until quitting time anyway, not that he ever punched a time clock.

After telling Carla his plans, Chase left for the day.

"SO I THINK THE REAL issue is, do you love my grandson?"

Miranda hadn't been prepared for the question and she stared at Leroy, who sat on a chaise longue in his great room, where he had a fantastic view of the land-scaped backyard.

"I…" She stuttered and shut her mouth. She certainly hadn't anticipated this question when she'd arrived at the McDaniel estate an hour ago.

The nurse had indicated it was fine for Miranda to visit, so long as she didn't cause Leroy any undue stress.

Causing him stress certainly wasn't her intention.

If anything, she was the one freaking out. Leroy

appeared to be calm and serene. Though he'd lost weight, his skin color was healthy and his eyes were sharp, as always. It had been great visiting, up until he'd dropped his question like a bomb.

"I can tell you're rather shocked," Leroy said. He adjusted the light throw covering his legs.

"I just wondered if it's your feelings for Chase that have made you so upset," he continued.

"I'm not upset," Miranda protested. And where had this come from? She and Leroy had been discussing the fall festival.

Leroy's hand trembled as he reached for his cup of water, a sign he still had recovering to do. "Ah, but you are. I could tell as soon as I saw you."

"Well, it's not because I love Chase." Miranda managed to force the words out. No way could she be in love with Leroy's grandson. "We snap at each other and get on each other's nerves. He resents me for the position you gave me. He usurps my authority."

"I figured that would happen the moment the doctors and my grandkids told me I couldn't work for a while. I knew he'd march in and take over. Are you going to let him?"

She'd gotten comfortable talking to Leroy since Chase had left, but this question she avoided. "Your family doesn't intend for you to go back."

"I know that, too. It doesn't surprise me a bit. They've lost both parents and all their grandparents but me. And I'm eighty. They have every reason to be overprotective. Doesn't mean I'm going to let them bully me around, though."

The nurse entered and Leroy let her check his blood pressure. She also refilled his water cup. "It's for my health. Doctor's orders. And I plan to be around to hold my next great-grandchild. Cecilia's getting close."

"I saw her at the hospital. She looks very pregnant."

"Don't remember much of that weekend, but the doc says that's okay. I remember everything else from my life, or at least the good parts, so that's all that counts. Have you considered the reason you and Chase get on each other's nerves might be because you belong together?"

"Really, I don't think so."

"No? I disagree. Did I ever tell you about my wife? Heidi lived on the next farm over. We'd grown up together. But let me assure you, we weren't childhood sweethearts. No sirree. She and I fought over everything. See, she was smart and so was I, and there could be only one high school valedictorian. I was certain it would be me. Sure didn't plan to let her win. Wasn't going to lose to a girl."

Miranda nodded. She had no idea where Leroy was going with this, but she found his story fascinating.

"Now, at the time the war was going on. The end of it, sure, but the Japanese hadn't surrendered. I was too young to enlist. My father also needed my help with the farm. We actually had a little money, so my mom hired Heidi to watch my little brother—you met Harvey— and do some of the cooking and cleaning. Both of Heidi's older brothers died fighting for the cause.

"But Heidi, boy, she held her head up. She refused to look at her job or our buying their farm and letting her family stay there as pity. And you know what? That girl who I used to throw worms at, whose tongue could be barbed wire, ended up being the love of my life. She covered her crush by being ornery and rude. Luckily, I wised up before I threw away what was right in front of my nose. I called her bluff."

"So who was valedictorian?" Miranda asked.

"She was. I failed a final in my math class. I didn't have time to study, since I had to get the spring planting done. Took a high B+ in the class."

"And she gloated."

Leroy chuckled. "Oh no. She yelled at me that I'd failed on purpose. I kissed her, told her she was going to marry me, and well, look how it all worked out."

"You're a cocky man, Leroy."

"Yeah." He grinned, and Miranda could see where Chase got his smile. "I could be bold when I wanted. Funny how life works. My mortal enemy the love of my life. So back to my grandson. I've seen the way he looks at you."

"With malice?"

Leroy shook his head. "No, I've seen true hate. His eyes certainly don't contain that. It's something very different altogether, and it's not the way he's looked at other women, either. Maybe you two ought to have a heart-to-heart. Clear the air. See if you can find some common ground."

"Perhaps," Miranda replied, not wanting to tell Leroy that it was far too late for that.

He fingered the throw. "Did you know that Heidi earned a scholarship because she was valedictorian? She attended college. Became a teacher. She taught for a few years before we had Chase's father. Heidi was worth failing a test for, that was for sure. Besides, I didn't need that money. I was going to be a farmer and build a company."

The sly fox. "So she was right. You duped her."

Leroy's eyes twinkled. "No. I took myself out of the running and gave her what she needed. In return, she gave me the best years of my life. No man could have been happier."

There was a lesson in his words, Miranda was sure, but figuring out exactly what Leroy was trying to tell her would have to wait, because the front door slammed and Chase strode into the room.

Leroy must have been wrong. Chase's face could reflect pure hate. And rage.

He didn't even attempt to hide his anger. "What the hell are *you* doing here?"

"CHASE!" The rebuke came not from Miranda but from his grandfather. "That is no way to greet one of my guests!"

Chase shouldn't have been surprised. In Leroy's book, you defended all women, even if they were wolves in sheep's clothing.

Chase quickly assessed the older man. He seemed fine. Frail, yes, but otherwise okay.

"She's not a guest," Chase responded, tempering his volume. "She's an employee and one determined to take over our company."

"This is my house, and if I say she's a guest, then she is. As for taking over the company, you seem to be the one doing that."

Chase's scowl deepened. "Not if Walter Peters gets his way."

Leroy's lips pursed. "What's he got to do with anything?"

"He's presenting a motion to the board on Monday to force me back on vacation and leave Miranda in charge."

Leroy adjusted his covers. "Oh? Is that all? Well, maybe that's a good idea."

Miranda sat there, swiveling her head left to right as if watching Ping-Pong. "I'll leave you two to discuss this."

Chase's glare pinned her to the seat. "Admit you know about Walter's motion."

Her chin came up slightly. "I do. But that's not what Leroy and I were talking about or why I came here." She faced his grandfather. "Walter told me his plan earlier today. It was his idea."

"Which I'm sure you were thrilled about," Chase retorted.

"Walter's a curmudgeon, that's for sure." Only Leroy didn't seem too perturbed by the current events. "I think you two should talk about this. No better time than the present." He rang a little bell and his nurse appeared. "I think I'd like to go to my room," he told her.

"I'll get your wheelchair," she said.

"I can help you," Chase offered, immediately concerned. He shouldn't even be discussing business. He'd promised his siblings. But trust Miranda to come here and try to shore up her position. When he'd seen her car in the driveway, he'd known exactly what she was doing.

"You're wrong. Leroy, this is not going to work. I'm leaving now," Miranda replied. Without waiting for either man's approval, she darted out.

"You ran her off," Leroy accused as the front door slammed.

"Me?" Chase couldn't believe his grandfather's protectiveness of Miranda. "Don't tell me she's got you under some kind of a spell. You can't side with her over your own family."

"Who says I'm siding with anyone?" Leroy snapped. "I wanted you to go away for a year to make up your mind about what was truly important. First chance you get, you're right back here."

"You had a heart attack. Where else would I be?"

"Well, I'm better now."

"No, you aren't," Chase argued. "You're eighty, whether you like it or not, and you have to take care of yourself."

"I've been taking care of myself for years. It's you who needs to take care of himself, Chase. You need to figure out what you want, what will bring you joy in life."

"I want to be CEO."

Leroy shook his head. "And that's it?"

"What else would there be?" Chase asked. Leroy had totally lost him. "I don't want to see McDaniel go into the wrong hands."

"Miranda isn't the 'wrong hands.' She doesn't have any stock options for two years. She earns a flat salary, which as this is low-cost-of-living Chenille, is less than she could have gotten by staying in Chicago. Any bonuses are paid exclusively on performance and need board approval. She has no vested interest in running the company into the ground. She won't even see a raise for six months."

Chase hated when his grandfather was right. Still… "She has no vested interest at all. Not like I do. Not only do I have stock, but it's my last name on the letterhead and the building."

"Isn't there a way for both of you to work together?" Leroy asked.

"Not when she's staging a coup."

Leroy's eyes narrowed and he waved away the wheelchair. "Give us a few more minutes. This job is that important to you?"

"I'm good at it. This is what I want, more than anything."

"Even if it means never finding the love of your life?"

Okay, this was a different tactic. Chase leaned back, trying to figure out where Leroy was going with all this. "What's that have to do with anything?"

"Running a company is nonstop, especially one that has your name on the door and the letterhead."

Chase knew that. "So?"

"You may never find love. You've always said you won't settle for less."

He squirmed. "Then I'll deal with it. If I don't have any kids, there's always my nieces and nephews. I'm sure some of them will be interested in business. I'm not sacrificing anything."

Leroy didn't look convinced. "You'd be a bachelor the rest of your days."

Chase bristled. "It's not like I can't find a date if I want one. I'm sure I could find a wife, too, if I need one that badly. You're the guy who's always called me a playboy."

"Perhaps you were once, but you shouldn't give up on finding the love of your life."

"I'm not sure there is such a thing."

Leroy frowned. "It exists. I had it."

"I meant for me," Chase clarified. Although he didn't like admitting it, maybe it was true. Maybe he was destined to be a bachelor for the rest of his life.

Leroy's eyes shone with pity. "That's sad."

Chase made a fist and then uncurled his hand. "I'm being realistic. It's a sacrifice I'm willing to make. You've always taught me to sacrifice for my family."

His grandfather shook his head. "I never taught you that. No one should give up true love. Our family would be fine without you as CEO of the company." Leroy remained silent for a moment before saying,

"Was there a reason you came by today other than to tell me about Walter?"

"I wasn't here to tell you about work at all. It's hot outside and I need to exercise. I came by to swim."

"Ah. You should get to it then." Leroy rang the bell and the nurse appeared instantly with his wheelchair. She must have been waiting outside the door.

Chase watched his grandfather's exit. How many times could a man screw up in a day? First Miranda, now Leroy. Monday couldn't come soon enough.

If he did get voted out, at least the torment would be over. He headed to the pool, changed into his trunks and dived in.

LEROY'S BEDROOM overlooked the backyard, so he knew that for the last hour Chase had been tearing up and down the pool as if training for the Olympics.

It saddened Leroy that his grandson couldn't see what was beneath his nose. Chase had finally met his perfect match, and he was about to toss his chance at love away because of his stubborn pride.

Leroy couldn't let him do that. He reached for his phone and dialed a number he knew by heart. "Hi, Walter," he said. "It's Leroy. What's this I hear about a motion?"

THERE WAS NO WAY she could be in love with Chase McDaniel.

Absolutely no way.

But ever since leaving the estate, Miranda hadn't been able to get the conversation out of her head. She'd replayed it over and over, analyzing Leroy's words from every angle.

She was not in love with Chase.

The lady doth protest too much, methinks. The line

from *Hamlet* had been one of her catch phrases since her junior year of high school. She was denying what she felt for Chase because she feared risking her heart.

Like Leroy and his beloved Heidi, she and Chase got on each other's nerves because they were fighting for the same thing. They had connected in the most fundamental way possible, and the result had been earth-shattering. But they were so busy proving who was better, warring to be named McDaniel's CEO, that they'd each missed the truth.

She was worth failing a test for, that was for sure. Besides, I was going to be a farmer.

The full meaning of Leroy's words suddenly became clear. He'd stepped out of Heidi's way. Was that what he thought she should do for his grandson—especially if she had fallen in love with him?

After what he'd said to Chase, Miranda wasn't certain of anything.

A knock sounded on her apartment door and she looked out the peephole.

Chase.

"Come on, Miranda. I know you're in there because your car is outside. We need to talk. Open up." He paused. "Please."

She slid the chain free and turned the knob. Chase's hair was damp, as if he'd just climbed out of the pool or the shower. He wore shorts and a T-shirt and looked damn sexy.

She couldn't love him. He was a cad. A jerk. An insensitive boor. Yet when they'd made love she'd felt complete for the first time. "I don't think this is a good idea."

"We have to find some common ground before

Monday or the company is going to end up in civil war," Chase said. "Please."

"Okay." She held the door open and let him step through. Her apartment was basic, just a one bedroom unit in a small, four-building complex. "Can I get you something to drink?"

"Do you mind? I really could use some water. I've just finished swimming."

Her kitchen was visible, separated from the living-dining area by a breakfast counter. While Chase took a seat on one of the bar stools, Miranda filled a glass from the water dispenser on the refrigerator. "Here."

"Thanks." He took a long sip. "My grandfather was pretty upset. You and I need to come to some sort of agreement."

She squared her shoulders. "If you're asking me to step down, I won't."

Chase sipped more water. "Well, I won't, either."

It figured. "Then we're at an impasse." Looking for a distraction she turned around and began straightening her kitchen towels.

"What is it for you? Why this particular company? I have lots of friends. I can find you a corporate job somewhere else, perhaps a start-up where you can get in from the very beginning if you want. Big or small, you name it."

She whirled around, towel in hand. "You're trying to buy me off?"

"It's obvious from today that we can't work together," Chase stated. "If it's about money, let me know. I have a trust fund. Name your price."

"You can't buy me. I'm not for sale."

He ran a hand through his damp hair. "I still think you're taking the situation personally. This is business.

This is what I've wanted ever since I was little. I promised myself when my dad died that I would helm McDaniel and I would do a good job. You can't take that from me."

"What about what I want? This is also my chance. I want to fulfill my parents' dreams, too."

"You'll have other chances. There are dozens of companies that would snatch you up. I'm a McDaniel. Where am I supposed to go? McDonald's? Kraft? It's not fitting."

His argument was reasonable, but coupled with her own doubts, and the cryptic advice Leroy had given her, she couldn't take any more. Already her head was about to explode. "I really think you should leave now."

He drained the water and stood. "Promise to think about it."

"I won't promise you anything."

He threw his arms up. "Look, I'm really sorry things got this far. We never should have made love, and my grandfather never should have concocted this ridiculous idea. Unfortunately, we can't take anything back. Just think about my offer. And, please, don't go see Leroy again. He had to go back to bed after we left. I don't want the situation between us to cause him grief."

She couldn't help herself. Chase had tried to buy her off, and trashed the night they'd shared. He'd gone for the jugular, and she wouldn't let him get away with it. "You're the one causing him grief. You're the one disappointing him."

His eyes widened. "Me? Hardly."

"Oh, there you go. Mr. Perfect. All he wants is for you to be happy. Instead you take the first opportunity to throw his gift back in his face. Did you ever think that the only thing he really wants is for you to be happy, like he was? Work doesn't keep you warm at night."

Chase's face paled, proving she'd hit a nerve. But there was no turning back now.

"Do you know what we were talking about when you arrived and jumped to the wrong conclusion?" she asked. "We were talking about your grandmother and how they met. Did you know he failed a test so that she'd be valedictorian in high school?

"Your grandfather loved your grandmother," Miranda declared, when Chase remained silent. "She was more important to him than fleeting glory. He also knew she needed the college scholarship. No wonder you're such a big disappointment to him. You sacrifice for your family, but you want recognition for being a martyr."

"I do not, and I don't have to stand here and take this." Chase strode to the front door and opened it. Miranda followed on his heels.

"No, you don't have to take it. But you should do a little thinking yourself this weekend. About what you're going to do if the board backs me instead of you."

He stood outside on her stoop. "That will never happen."

She couldn't contain her reaction. Upset with the stupid feelings she'd had for this man, she needed to lash out. "We'll see what unfolds on Monday. You stand a good chance of losing."

"Don't get your hopes up, because I highly doubt it. You're forgetting who I am."

She planted her hands on her hips. "Oh, I know exactly who you are. A high-and-mighty fool who's about to take a fall."

He had the gall to laugh. "Not going to happen."

"Wrong. And let me tell you something you can take to the bank. I don't love you."

He looked as if she'd smacked him in the face. "What?"

She hadn't intended to blurt out anything Leroy had said, but it was too late now. She tried to regroup and calm her frazzled nerves. She could not let Chase read anything more into this than it was. Which was nothing.

"Your grandfather asked me if I love you. For some reason he thinks you and I should be all happily ever after. As if I would want to be with a man like you."

Chase clamped his arms across his chest. "He asked you that."

It was either be mean or cry. She couldn't show him how hurt she was. "He did. I hated to disillusion him. I'm sure you do that enough."

A strange expression crossed Chase's face. "He thinks you're in love with me."

"You wish," she said, and then the weight of the day came crashing down and she did the first thing that came to mind. She ended the conversation by slamming the door.

CHASE WALKED DOWN the steps and headed to his car. He wasn't sure what he'd expected when he'd arrived at her apartment. He certainly hadn't foreseen what she'd hurled at him last.

His grandfather thought Miranda was in love with him.

Surely that had to be the dumbest idea Leroy had ever come up with. But somehow it made sense. Chase felt as if he'd found the missing puzzle pieces he needed to have a complete picture.

He drove back over to his grandfather's. Leroy was

sitting in the great room again. "I don't want to get into it," he warned.

"Neither do I," Chase replied. "I just have a question for you. It's about Miranda. Why did you ask her if she was in love with me?"

Leroy put his magazine down. "Because you two look at each other the way Heidi and I did."

Chase sank into a nearby armchair and absorbed that. He felt numb, as if he'd been the world's biggest fool. "So Miranda hasn't made any declarations?"

"No. She thinks you hate her. Why should she?"

"No reason," Chase said quickly.

Leroy shook his head. "Like nothing happened on those late nights at the lake? You two didn't have a little fun on the dock?"

His head shot up. "What did you see?"

Leroy grinned. "Thanks for confirming my suspicions."

Chase groaned. So much for being discreet. Leroy had gotten him with the oldest trick in the book.

But instead of gloating, his grandfather sighed. He didn't revel in discovering the truth. "I'm an old man. We get up a lot in the middle of the night to go to the bathroom. While I didn't see anything, it's pretty easy to figure out something's going on when the boat's missing and the boathouse light is on until the wee hours of the morning. I guessed you weren't down there by yourself."

"I'm very attracted to her. We got involved."

"It's good for you to admit it. Everyone else can see how you look at her. Why do you think I kept trying to push you two together?"

"But it can't work. We're both after the same job. It's

not something we can share. One of us has to go. And I don't want it to be me."

Leroy tapped his fingers on the chair. "I see."

Chase stood. "I just wanted you to know."

"So do you love her?"

Chase froze. "When I first met her I had this wild idea that she could be the one. But I've learned things aren't always what they seem."

"They often aren't. But sometimes they are."

Chase shook his head. "Not in this case. I'll abide by whatever decision the board makes on Monday. I don't want to cause you any more stress or give you any more reasons to be disappointed in me."

"I'm not disappointed. I never have been. I love you. Always will."

Chase nodded, his shoulders relaxing a little. "I appreciate that. I'll come by sometime tomorrow and check on you."

"I'm not made of glass. And Chris is coming to stay for the weekend. I got a new crossword book."

Crossword puzzles were Leroy and Chris's thing. "Okay then. I'll call you."

Chase was almost to the foyer before his grandfather called his name. Chase paused. Leroy looked so small sitting in his chair, and Chase got a sense of just how frail and precious life really was.

"Your father would be very proud of you, Chase. Remember, this isn't about doing the right thing for the family. It's about doing what makes you happy. I had it all. So can you."

"Somehow I doubt that."

"I don't. Now, go home and drive safe. Oh, and Chase? Admit the truth to yourself."

Chase frowned. "About what?"

"That you love her."

He laughed shortly. "It wouldn't matter even if I did."

Leroy shook his head and gave a small, sad smile. "Get your priorities straight. That's what this year was supposed to be about. Love is all that matters."

Yeah, right, Chase thought as he drove home. Love might be all that mattered, but love also broke your heart. He'd loved his parents and they'd died. Love brought pain.

As for Miranda, too many harsh things had been said between them to make things okay. You could glue together a broken glass, but it wouldn't hold water.

Even if he loved her—which he didn't, he added quickly—all they'd had was great sex. He liked the way her short black hair lay against her cheek after lovemaking. He adored the way her lips were puffy after a long, passionate kiss. He remembered how she felt in his arms and wanted her there again. He'd probably never stop wanting her.

But you couldn't build a relationship on that. Hell, they couldn't even work together without arguing. Any relationship between them was doomed. Come Monday, one of them would stand and one of them would fall.

He prayed he'd be the one left standing, and as he did, he suddenly understood where his grandfather had been leading him.

Buildings and letterhead didn't keep you warm at night. Miranda Craig was probably the love of his life. Chase might win and be named CEO, but he was going to lose something priceless.

Chapter Thirteen

Chase resisted the urge to loosen his tie. He'd been in the hot seat for the past ten minutes.

"Chase, you have no real experience," Walter said. As soon as the meeting began, he'd made his proposal to remove him.

"Neither does Miranda," Chase replied as he glanced around the conference room. About half the board members were nodding in agreement. "She's been here a little over seven weeks. I've been here nineteen years counting my part-time employment during high school."

"That's true," Kathleen Kennedy pointed out. The president of the board, she'd been the one solidly in Chase's corner from the very start of the meeting. "Walter, we know you've trained Miranda well, and you favor her because she's your protégée, but this is McDaniel Manufacturing and Chase is heir apparent. What type of message would it send if we went over his head and replaced him with an outsider, and an in-experienced one at that? It's not as if he's incompetent."

"True," Nick Cissna agreed.

As much as he wanted, Chase didn't squirm. Being

dissected and discussed wasn't very pleasant, but it was a necessary part of the process.

Kathleen continued. "Chase met with Mike Storm and the governor Friday afternoon regarding Rhodes Printing perhaps choosing Chenille for their expansion. He's already leading this company. I spoke with Mike on Saturday and he said Chase played an instrumental role. Everyone was very impressed."

"Did anyone ask Miranda to be at that meeting? Where is she, anyway?" Logan Bennett asked.

"She was hired to be vice president, not CEO. I'm ahead of her in my grandfather's chain of command," Chase replied. As for the second question, he'd expected Miranda to be in attendance. "I haven't seen her in the office since Thursday."

"She should be here," Nick stated.

Everyone looked at Walter, who shrugged. "I have no idea where she is. I spoke with her last night at length and expected her to be present. Maybe she had car trouble."

"Considering the importance of this meeting, she should have called." Kathleen folded her hands on the table in front of her. "We've been here a half hour with no word. Unless there's anything else, shall we vote? It's basically Miranda or Chase. My vote goes to Chase."

"Miranda," Walter said.

Chase watched as two more people voted for him. There were twelve board members total. Two were absent—Jake Palenske and Leroy McDaniel. The vote was five-two in Chase's favor when the door to the boardroom opened.

Chase frowned. No one ever disturbed a board meeting. No one would be allowed inside except for…

"Sorry I'm late," Leroy said as his nurse wheeled him in. "Over there," he told her, and she helped him into an empty conference table chair before leaving. He glanced around the table. "What'd I miss?"

Chase gripped his seat to keep himself from standing. His grandfather was not supposed to be leaving the house except to go to the doctor. He wasn't well enough yet. He'd been forbidden to stress himself with work, yet here he was.

"We were voting. Chase has five. Miranda has two," Kathleen said.

Leroy nodded. "Ah. So if I vote for Miranda and everyone left follows what I choose…"

"Then she'd be our new CEO until you return," Kathleen replied, not looking too pleased with his interruption.

Leroy drew himself up. "Oh, I have to return. Not that I'll stay past next May. I promised Chase that he'd be CEO after his one-year leave of absence, if that is what he really wants. I'm not retracting that promise."

"Then what is going on?" Kathleen asked. "You told us Chase wanted this vacation. Are you saying you forced him to go on sabbatical?"

Leroy had the decency to look sheepish. "I did. Call it the eccentricity of an old man. I wanted Chase to have a year to find out if he really wanted to fill my shoes. He's been here since it's been legal for him to work."

The old man glanced down the table at his grandson. "Have you ever worked for anyone else?"

"No," Chase said. Once again Leroy had thrown a wrench into the cogs. This also couldn't be good.

"I wanted to give him a choice. Taking over McDaniel shouldn't be an obligation, but a well thought out decision."

The board members began nodding, agreeing with Leroy. Chase managed not to wince.

"I would say we know where you stand, Chase," Logan said, and everyone swiveled to look in Chase's direction. "You want to be CEO."

He tried to project a calm and self-assured demeanor. "I do. I definitely want to take over when my grandfather retires. I will admit that I didn't want this vacation, but I agreed to it since it was so important to Leroy."

Chase turned his attention to his grandfather. "My brother and sisters are not going to be happy you're here. You're supposed to be resting."

Leroy shrugged. "Which I'll do later. Obviously, I'd like to have Miranda continue on in the interim, and send Chase back on his vacation."

Chase's cheek twitched, but he managed to remain still and not interrupt.

"However, I can see how impossible that is," Leroy continued. "Chase clearly wants to be here, and that's what I wanted him to figure out for himself. Besides, naming Miranda CEO is a moot point."

Leroy had dressed for the board meeting. He'd donned one of his best suits, and now he reached into his jacket pocket and removed an envelope.

"Miranda came by the house this morning and gave me her notice. In turn, I offered her a year's pay as severance and released her from her duties effective today. Since she was hired to do Chase's job, and he's here, there's no reason for her to remain at McDaniel Manufacturing."

There were gasps, but Chase hardly heard them. His entire focus was on his grandfather, and vice versa. It was as if the two of them were the only ones in the room. Miranda had resigned. She'd quit. The announcement hit Chase like a punch to the gut.

"Chase is here and he wants this job. I'd be remiss

if I turned him down. He's family and he's earned it," Leroy stated, finally breaking eye contact.

He glanced around the table. "Let's vote and make it official that Chase is the new CEO of McDaniel Manufacturing. I'll stay on in an advisory capacity until December 31. Congrats, Chase. You got what you wanted."

So why did it feel so awful?

"Okay," Kathleen said, ready to regain control over the vote. She seemed rattled, but determined to get this over with. "All those in favor of Chase McDaniel being named CEO?"

Everyone but Walter and Leroy raised their hands. Kathleen pinned her attention on the two men. "All opposed?" There was no opposition, as both men chose to abstain. "Motion carries. Congratulations, Chase." She sighed. "If there's nothing else?"

After a quick motion to adjourn, the boardroom emptied. Everyone appeared to be relieved that the nightmare was over, and each member shook Chase's hand and congratulated him before leaving.

"So she resigned?" Walter asked when only he and the McDaniels remained.

Leroy grimaced. "I warned you not to push her. She came to see me this morning, and I couldn't talk her out of it. Her mind was made up. Said she talked to you last night, did some soul searching and knew what she really wanted and needed to do."

Walter whirled on Chase, his tone accusatory. "What did you do to her? What did you say?"

"Nothing," he said defensively. "The last time I saw her she planned on being here and giving me a run for my money. I haven't seen her since Thursday, like I said. I don't know why she changed her mind."

"She told me her reasons were personal. I left it at that and suggest we all do," Leroy said. "So, Walter, since I've sprung the coop, how about we go get some lunch before my nurse calls time?"

"Okay," he agreed. "But only if we go to Maxine's. I'm dying for a piece of her cherry pie."

Leroy turned to his grandson. "Chase, I guess you ought to let Carla know the news. She'll need to contact PR and have an announcement sent to the press. If you have questions for me, you can stop by the house later tonight."

Leroy's nurse entered and Chase knew he'd been dismissed. "Just take it easy," he told his grandfather.

"Lucinda will make sure of that."

"I will," his nurse confirmed.

Carla had already heard the news by the time Chase arrived, and she beamed with excitement. "So it's final."

"Yep." But for some reason he didn't feel like celebrating. Still, he had to act the part for his staff. "I guess later this week we need to discuss your title and your raise."

She kept smiling. "That would be wonderful. Thank you."

Chase gave her a cheeky grin. "I'm no dummy. A man's only as good as his secretary."

"You'd better believe it." Carla laughed.

Chase entered his office and took a seat at his desk. He reached for a piece of paper and a pen. At the top he wrote "To do." Underneath he wrote "VP." Someone had to fill his spot. He'd have Carla ask personnel to send him company files of good internal candidates. He had some ideas already, as he'd been working with these people for years, but he didn't want to miss considering anyone.

Thinking of missing people, Chase rose and went

down to Miranda's office. Her secretary, Lauren, jumped to her feet when she saw him. "I hear congratulations are in order."

He nodded. "They are."

She stood there awkwardly. "You'll do a great job."

"Thanks. Has Miranda collected her belongings?"

Lauren frowned. "What do you mean? Her door's been shut all morning and she left me a voice mail saying she wouldn't be in."

"She resigned."

"Oh." Lauren sat back down, stunned.

"Don't worry, your job's safe and you'll be working with whomever we hire to take her place. But her quitting was unexpected. She told my grandfather just this morning."

Chase opened the door to Miranda's office. The place had been stripped bare. All of her personal touches had been removed. She must have acted quickly, before anyone arrived that morning.

Lauren came up behind him. "I had no idea she'd moved out."

"Neither did I," Chase admitted. He closed the door. "For now, anything you can't handle, send to Carla. She'll run point."

"Okay. But I can't believe Miranda would just leave like that."

Chase could, and as he headed for the parking lot, he called Carla and told her he'd return in a few hours. He had some questions he wanted answered.

MIRANDA COVERED HER HEAD with a pillow, but the banging on her front door wouldn't stop. Whoever it was wasn't going away.

She crawled out of bed and checked the clock. It

was almost noon, meaning she'd had about a three-hour nap.

Who knew resigning could be so draining? She certainly hadn't imagined this scenario. But as Sunday had come and gone, Miranda knew she couldn't handle the glee on Chase's face when he defeated her. She also knew she couldn't live with the results if she won. He'd hate her.

Around ten last night she'd come to her decision. She'd gone to her office, packed her belongings and had the weekend security guard carry them to her car. Like a thief in the night, she'd stolen away, revealing her crime only to Leroy this morning.

He'd read her letter, looked up with those blue eyes so like Chase's and said, "The answer to my question is yes, isn't it?"

She'd nodded and burst into tears.

"My grandson's a hard one, isn't he? So lovable, but so clueless and so stubborn. He has all my worst flaws. You sure I can't convince you to stay?"

"No. I need to leave." Miranda had replied. Since Chase obviously was unable to share his playground, she knew he'd never be able to give her his heart. She couldn't work with him, feeling the way she did. You weren't supposed to fall in love with a man who'd never love you back.

Leroy had reached over and patted her hand. "I feel like I'm buying you out of my grandson's life. Let me tell you, I never wanted this when I hired you."

"I know. It's my own fault." It was. She'd asked Chase to go boating that fateful night. She'd assumed it would just be sex and chemistry. When it wasn't, she'd figured she'd have a year to get over him. She'd gambled with her heart and lost.

She could have said no, right? But she hadn't.

Miranda wiped away her tears and took a steadying breath. The banging on her door had ceased for a few seconds, only to resume. She probably looked like hell, but who cared? By tomorrow she planned on being as far from Chenille as possible. Miranda felt a bit like Sabrina having "won" a ticket to Paris. Only Linus Larrabee wasn't going to come tell her he'd made a mistake.

Miranda made it to the front door and glanced through the peephole, then turned around and pressed her back against it.

"I can hear you moving around in there," Chase called.

He was the last person she wanted to see. Did he have to come and gloat? Couldn't he just leave her alone? "Go away."

He knocked again. "No. I want to talk to you."

"Well, I don't want to talk to you."

"I'll knock all day," he threatened.

She knew he would. "I'll call the cops and have them arrest you."

"Go ahead. It won't do you any good. I went to high school with half of them and McDaniel is a key donor to their police officers' fund. I'm not leaving until you talk to me."

She drew a hand through her tousled hair. Damn the man. She could picture a scene with Chase and the cops laughing at her expense. Everyone in this town sided with him.

She held her hand up to her mouth and breathed into it as Chase started pounding on the door again. Her breath wasn't too bad, and it wasn't as if she was going to kiss him. That's how she'd gotten into this mess in the first place. She turned around and unlocked the door.

"Finally," Chase said as she let him in. His gaze raked over her.

"Don't say I look like hell," she warned. "I'm not in any mood to deal with you."

His brow creased. "I thought you saw my grandfather this morning."

"I did. I came home and crawled back under the covers." She closed the door to keep the heat from invading her air-conditioned apartment. "If you came to gloat, do me a favor, consider it done and go."

"I'm not here for that." He reached up and loosened his tie. "I came by to see why you resigned. The last time we talked I thought you were all fired up to be CEO. You sure gave me that impression."

"Is that why you're here? To figure out why I gave in? Do you have to know everything?"

He nodded. "In this case, yes."

"You said it was business. Your being here is personal."

"Damn it! Stop twisting my words. Yes, I'm McDaniel's new CEO. But I didn't expect you to quit. In fact, Leroy showed up and planned to vote for you. You would have won."

A little more of her heart broke. "Chase, don't you realize that you're a force of nature? No one wins against you. Sometimes it's better to forfeit. It's better to fold than play a losing hand until you're broke."

He scowled. "You aren't a quitter."

He had her there. "No, I'm not. But I got a better offer. Your grandfather gave me a year off with full pay. You were right. I was jealous of you and your forced vacation. Well, I took the offer your grandfather made you. This is my chance to see the world."

"Then why do you look like you've been crying for the past two days?"

She glared at him. "Because I just woke up, that's why. I stayed up late, packing my office things, and I'm tired. I have belongings to store. Don't think you're worth shedding tears over, because you're not."

He held up his hands in protest. "Okay. I can see you're still a little testy about all this."

"And you're still a jerk of the first order. Do you practice it? From the moment we met you've been condescending and crass."

"I have not. You had a flat tire. I tried to help. You were the one who snapped at me. I never assumed you were incompetent."

Her shoulders sagged. "Arguing gets us nowhere. That's why I can't work for you. It's what we always do."

"Not always." His gaze held hers. "I remember things we did that were much better than fighting."

She remembered, too, which was the problem. He'd stolen her heart, and he didn't even know it.

Chase reached for her hand. "I never meant for it to go down this way. All I wanted was to be CEO. I'd be happy to have you work for McDaniel. Come back."

She pulled away. "Chase, how can I look at you on a daily basis? If I'd known I was going to have to do that I wouldn't have made love to you."

"So you admit you have feelings for me."

"Oh, I have feelings all right, just not the kind you're hoping for."

Chase sighed. "You have so many walls raised. You wear your goals and dreams like a shield. You don't let anyone inside. You know what I think? You're going to be exactly like me. You'll be going stir-crazy after two weeks. You'll pinch pennies instead of going five stars. You'll worry that you're losing time to find another job. You may go to Paris, but you won't enjoy it. You'll be too busy stressing."

"I don't think so, Chase. Unlike you, I know how to relax. I really think you should leave. It's best we don't talk any more. You got what you wanted." She reached behind her and opened the door. The hot air rushed in.

Chase shook his head. "To you it might seem like I got what I wanted. But I didn't, not really. I sacrificed something very important."

"Yeah, right."

He stepped closer and put a hand under her chin. "I had to choose between my company and you."

"As if you really spent any time thinking about that." Chase truly knew how to rub salt into a wound. "Please, just leave."

"Not until you tell me where you're going."

"Somewhere far away from here. Somewhere I can start fresh. Now, leave."

He ran a fingertip over her lower lip. "I never wanted to hurt you."

Didn't he know his very presence hurt her? She stepped out of his reach. "Go."

He didn't move. "If that's what you really want."

What she wanted was for the pain to stop. She needed to pick up the pieces of her heart and heal. He'd never love her. His job came first.

"It's what I want. Go, Chase. I'm sure you have work to do."

He hesitated before saying, "Yeah, I probably do. Goodbye, Miranda."

She held on to the door, not trusting her voice to get

the words out without cracking. She had to move on. He went down a few steps, and as he turned around for one final look, she let her dreams die, and closed the door.

Chapter Fourteen

Don Henley had a song with a line saying something about work not keeping you warm. As Chase replayed "The Heart of the Matter" on his iPod for the tenth time during his nightly jog, he realized what was bugging him.

Sacrifices sucked.

It had been a month since he'd been named CEO. In that time he'd worked ten-hour days, except for a one-day trip he'd taken to see Cecilia's baby, and he'd worked his body into even leaner shape.

He'd drop into bed each night exhausted, but he never really slept. Instead, he replayed every moment he and Miranda had spent together. It hadn't taken him long to realize he'd made the dumbest mistake of his life. He'd let her go.

But there was no way to have her and be CEO. He'd been over every possible solution.

He, Chase McDaniel, would not have his Heidi, as his grandfather had. Chase's role was to build the company into something his nieces and nephews would want to run, or at least into something he could sell one day and set the entire family up for life.

He had to be content with that. Tomorrow was Friday, and he'd taken the day off so he and his grandfather could go to Lone Pine. Leroy had been going stir-crazy in Chenille and wanted to visit the lake one last time before they closed the lodge for the winter. The doctor had agreed with the trip, so long as Leroy had a nurse nearby just in case.

Chase hadn't been to the lake since the weekend with Miranda. He knew it would only make him miss her more. The caretaker had long ago cleaned up any mess left in the haste of getting Leroy to the hospital, so Chase had had no reason to return.

If all went well, next year Leroy would spend the entire summer at the lodge, having handed over the reins to Chase. So far the transition was going smoothly. An interim vice president was in place and Chase worked well with her. The next meeting with Rhodes Printing was a few weeks away, when company representatives and Iowa officials would arrive in town for a site visit.

Chase reached his house and went inside to shower and pack. He'd hired a limo so that he, Leroy and the nurse could travel in greater comfort. His phone rang and he picked it up.

"Making sure nothing's changed," Leroy said.

Chase held the phone against his ear with his shoulder and stripped off his shorts. "Not on my end."

"Walter and his wife are meeting us there. They'll be in the cottage."

This was a surprise. While Walter did normally spend a week at the lake, Chase had thought this year would be different, since Leroy was in Chenille. Maybe that's why his grandfather had been so insistent on heading to Lone Pine this weekend.

"Chase?"

"I'm here," he replied. "I'll see you tomorrow at seven."

"You will be able to handle Walter, won't you? He was rather harsh last time you saw him."

Chase answered with a question. "Have I been doing a good job?"

His grandfather sighed. "You've gone above and beyond everyone's expectations."

"Then it'll all be fine," Chase said. He made himself a promise not to ask about Miranda. She'd told him to go, and he had. Everything they'd had was in the past.

So why did his heart still hurt?

As the sun dipped below the horizon, ending yet another Friday, Miranda tightened her grip on the steering wheel. She shouldn't be here. She'd sworn she'd never come back.

But she'd been in Minneapolis–Saint Paul retrieving her car, close enough that she couldn't say no to two people who meant the world to her.

After leaving Chenille, she'd put her car in long-term parking and flown to Vancouver, Canada. She'd spent the past month at a high-end wilderness resort, isolated from the rest of the world, basically licking her wounds.

Sadly, Chase had been right. After the first few days, she'd been antsy. By the time she left, she'd been stir-crazy. The resort was beautiful, a full five star establishment. She hadn't skimped on the money. But there were only so many yoga classes she could take, so many books she could read and so many hikes through the woods she could go on before Miranda longed for what she did best—work.

No wonder Chase had arrived home at the first opportunity. She'd relaxed, but she'd never been able to turn off that driven, alpha side of her personality. While being one with nature was enriching and enlightening, she didn't find just "being" very satisfying. She liked supervising things and solving problems. She needed to do something.

Her plan was to return to Chicago and start the job search. She'd save the rest of her severance for a rainy day. Despite what she'd told Chase in a fit of bravado, traveling the world could wait.

She reached the turnoff, and her tires crunched over the gravel that led to Lone Pine Lake. Walter and his wife were staying at the cottage, and she'd agreed to meet them and spend one night before continuing on to Chicago. When she'd spoken to them a few days ago to confirm, Walter had assured her that Leroy was doing quite well. Neither of them had mentioned Chase.

Still, her fingers grew even tighter on the wheel as she reached Lone Pine. In the distance she could see that a few lights were on in the lodge, but neither Chase's nor Leroy's car was parked out front. She loosened her grip. The McDaniels weren't here.

She parked next to Walter's car, turned off the engine and hopped out. Although she couldn't see them, she could hear Walter and his wife talking.

"Hey," she called.

"Ah, Miranda! We're in here." Christine answered from the porch. "Let me turn a light on."

"No need. Then the bugs will swarm. I can see well enough." Miranda knew the short path by heart, and soon pulled on the screen door and entered. Walter and his wife sat in Adirondack chairs, several citronella candles providing a romantic glow and protection against any insects that got through the screens. Both rose to their feet and hugged her.

"I'm so glad you didn't chicken out," Walter told her as he released her.

"I've missed you two," she replied.

"You didn't enjoy Canada?" Christine asked.

"It was lovely, but I'm ready to get back to work."

"I've heard about a company that needs a vice president," Walter said. "You'd be perfect for the job.

"You can tell me about it tomorrow. I'm pretty beat. I lost two hours, flying east, and I had to get up really early to catch my flight."

"Grab her bags, Walter," Christine insisted. The screen door banged as he left. "Are you doing okay?"

"I'm fine," Miranda lied. "It gets easier every day."

"Oh sweetie, I'm so sorry. Walter told me what happened. I never imagined you would fall for Chase. Do you still love him?"

Tired as she was, Miranda didn't even question how Walter knew about that. Leroy had probably told him. Hopefully, that was as far as the revelations went. "I don't know. I think I'm still grieving."

"That's understandable and so normal. My son is going through a divorce. It's horrible. At least you didn't marry the man."

"We were never like that," Miranda said. They hadn't even dated. They'd just had sex.

"Still…" Christine soothed. "Come inside. Your bed is all made up and you look exhausted. We were about to turn in anyway. We were just waiting for you."

Fifteen minutes later Miranda was settled in the room she'd stayed in her first time here. An hour later she was lying in bed, staring at the ceiling. While she was physically exhausted, being at Lone Pine brought back too many memories and emotions that kept her awake.

She clicked on the light and picked up the novel she was reading, but after staring at the page for several minutes, unseeing, gave up.

Tomorrow she was leaving. She might as well go down to the dock for one last visit. Maybe that would finally exorcise the demons and lay them and Chase to rest.

She slid out of bed and carried her flip-flops in her hand so she wouldn't wake Walter and Christine. The moon wasn't full, but there was enough light to see, and soon she was dangling her feet from the end of the pier.

A sense of peace had washed over her the minute she sat down. The world was still, except for nocturnal creatures searching for food and mates. Then she heard something else—the motor of a boat. She peered through the night, but didn't see anything. It was probably the sound of a fishing boat far out across the water. Lone Pine's runabout was gone, but she assumed the caretaker had put the craft in dry dock after she'd called about Leroy.

She lay back and folded her hands under her head so she could stare at the stars. Even Canada couldn't compare to this, and where she'd been the sky had been as close to heaven as one could get.

This place was magical. She sighed. She was going to miss coming here.

Water began to lap at the dock, and Miranda rose up on her elbows. The bow of a boat came into view about fifteen feet away. The craft was hugging the shoreline, and for a moment Miranda worried the driver wouldn't see the dock, since a big oak tree jutted from the point.

But the boat maneuvered around it smoothly and came closer. She realized why as the man on board grabbed the post at the end of the dock. The words left her mouth at the same time they left his.

"What are you doing here?"

"ME? I LIVE HERE." Chase stared. He'd been out on a night cruise, seeking solace. He certainly hadn't expected to find Miranda sitting on the dock like some water nymph. His libido slipped into overdrive and he tried to calm himself. Even in the shadows she was breathtaking. "And you?"

"I'm staying the night with Walter and Christine. Tomorrow I leave for Chicago." Her tone turned accusatory. "I didn't think you'd be here. Where's your car?"

"We hired a limo. Leroy needed the space to stretch out." Chase drew the boat alongside.

Miranda's jaw dropped. "He's here, too?"

Chase nodded. "For the weekend. We're closing up the house. And he wanted to visit with Walter."

"When did Walter learn you were coming?"

Chase shrugged. "I think they arranged this trip sometime last week."

"I don't believe it. Of all the sneaky things to do." Miranda jumped to her feet.

Chase killed the engine and tossed her the rope. "So what's going on?"

"Walter. He told me Leroy wasn't coming… No, I guess he didn't. I just assumed." She looped the rope, securing the runabout. "I'm sorry, but it seems as if Leroy and Walter are doing some matchmaking. Walter knew I was flying into Minnesota today and he insisted I come by and visit him and Christine. I didn't realize you would be here or I would have said no."

Chase hopped onto the dock. "You're a surprise to me as well." And not a bad one. He thought of her often. He missed her. And right now, in the soft moonlight, she was a vision. "How are you doing?"

"I'll be fine once I get out of here." She stepped forward, but Chase stood between her and the shore. He held his ground.

"Do you hate me that much?" he asked.

She waved him aside. "It's just better if we avoid each other."

"That day at my grandfather's, he suggested we talk. Perhaps our meeting here is a sign that we should."

"Oh Chase, what is there to talk about? Haven't we said all that needs to be said?"

The answer came to him in a flash. "No, we haven't. I was wrong."

She sighed and planted her hands on her hips. "Please don't start. You're never wrong. You know, I was bored in a week's time. There. I said it. I'm headed to Chicago to find a job. So don't. I'm already beating myself up enough with the fact that you were right."

He ran a finger down her forearm. She jerked, but not like someone who hated his touch. "I've missed you terribly."

She looked startled and her arms straightened. "You have? I don't believe you."

He captured her hand. Her skin was warm and soft. "Everyone in town constantly asks about you. They miss you, too."

She tried to pull away, but he held on tighter. "They'll get over it," she stated.

"*I* won't." He wished she'd believe him.

Her lower lip quivered and he hated that he'd hurt her. "Chase, don't lie. You were over me before your grandfather's heart attack. I saw the picture of you and that girl in Colorado."

Ah. That explained so much. Another missing puzzle piece dropped into place. "Is that why you're so mad?"

"I was never mad," she retorted.

He couldn't help himself; he smiled. "Liar. You were jealous."

"You need to stop thinking so highly of yourself. We had sex. It was nothing."

"If you really believe that then let's have sex again. Right here. Right now."

She sputtered and stared at him as if he were crazy. "That's ridiculous."

He pulled her into a tight embrace. He'd so missed holding her. "Why? We had really great sex. The best of my life. I haven't even kissed anyone since I last kissed you. As for the girl, we were hiking buddies on that trip, nothing more. So indulge me. Let's give ourselves another night to remember. After all, you're saying it's meaningless. So more pleasure for pleasure's sake shouldn't matter."

She shoved against him and he let her go. He'd pushed her far enough. He knew what she'd do, but still thanked the heavens when she reacted as he'd hoped.

"No. I'm not a piece of meat to be chewed up and spit out."

"You weren't then. Why would you be now?" Chase ran a finger down her arm again. Now they were getting somewhere. The first wall had cracked. She'd revealed her jealousy, meaning she cared. He'd learned that he'd hurt her—she thought he'd used her and cast her aside.

Even though she'd said she was okay with one night of sex, she really wasn't. Their lovemaking had been much more, and she was finally close to admitting that.

A flicker of hope flared to life and he pressed further. To have a chance, they were going to have to pull down all the walls between them. Through the physical they could get to the emotional. To the heart of the matter. To the truth—that they belonged together. "See how your body reacts to my touch?"

"Stop it. I'm not going to have sex with you again."

"Because our connection scares you."

She scowled. "I'm not scared."

"Oh yes, you are. Because the only time we've ever been honest with each other has been on this lake. I made a horrible mistake in letting you go. I'm not doing that ever again."

"I can't just have casual sex with you. I shouldn't have that night."

"Who said the sex would be casual? I didn't. That's not what I want, either. Don't you realize the reason we fight is because you and I have feelings for each other?"

"I can't do lust."

She was still missing the point. "I'd say what we feel for each other goes a lot deeper than that—much deeper, and far more serious."

Chase reached out and took her hands. She didn't pull away. "My grandfather said something that surprised me."

"What was that?" she whispered.

"He told me that you and I look at each other the way he and my grandma used to." Chase moved his thumb in a circle on her palm. "You never met Heidi, but to this day I can picture the love she shared with him."

"Oh, Chase, that's so not us."

"It could be," he said stubbornly.

She tried to free her hands but he held them tight.

"What will it take to make you believe me?" he asked. "I made the biggest mistake of my life. I don't want to make another one."

Her eyes widened. "You keep saying that."

"Well, it's true. I chose McDaniel. I chose my name on the company letterhead. I couldn't see any way to be CEO and still have you. So I lost you. It hurts to admit how stupid I was."

"You made the right decision. I would have done the same thing."

The night seemed to envelop them. Even the sounds of nature faded as she reassured him. She was so wonderful.

"No, you wouldn't. In fact, you didn't. You resigned instead. You sacrificed yourself and your dreams to make me happy, like my grandfather did for my grandmother when he failed that math test. Why would you do that? I can only think of one reason. It's the same reason I sacrifice for my family. Love."

"Chase…" Again she tugged. But he refused to let go, afraid she would disappear.

He shook his head. "Please let me finish. When I first saw you, I told myself you were someone worth knowing. It's like something inside of me knew you were the one I'd been waiting for. Then all this craziness with work started."

"We can't work together. We proved that."

"Yes, we *can* work together. We can do whatever we want if we put our minds to it. You and I belong together. You and I deserve a chance to see what we can become. My job has never made me as happy as I was with you, here, that one weekend."

Her mouth opened in protest. Oh, how he loved her lips. He loved everything about her. No sense in denying it. He'd found his soul mate.

"Lust. It blinds you," Miranda scoffed.

"Don't downplay what we had. It was special, unlike

anything else. I would trade my company to feel that way again."

"What way?"

"Whole. Complete. Content. In love."

MIRANDA TUGGED AGAINST his grip, but he still refused to let go. Didn't he see this would never work? She'd spent the last month trying to forget him and the fiasco with McDaniel. Now here he was, saying things that she'd never get over.

"Chase, you don't love me."

His eyes held hers. "And you know what's in my heart?"

Miranda faltered. Actually, she had no idea.

"Do you know what I gave up to be CEO?" Chase asked.

She was so tired, and emotionally wrought. Every day since he'd left for Colorado had been hell. "What?"

"I gave up true love."

He'd caught her off guard, but this time she got her hands free. "Please. Don't."

He reached for her again and she sidestepped. "Don't what? Tell you the truth? Tell you that I've fallen in love with you? Because that's the only explanation for the pain I've been in since you left."

"You don't know what love is," she said, still unable to believe.

His posture was strong and certain. "Oh, but trust me, I do. I've seen perfect examples in my siblings, my parents and my grandparents. The only time I've ever been overpowered by emotions I never experienced before has been with you. I overreact. I say things I don't mean. I want so much to knock down the walls you hide behind. I want you, but it's so much more than sex. I want a future, and for the first time in my life, I can't find a way to make that happen. Tell me, what do I have to do so we can be together?"

Tears came to her eyes. "I don't know."

He lifted her chin with his fingers and peered into her eyes. "It's about forgiveness. I love you. Please give me another chance."

She wanted to, but she'd been hurt before. Could she trust him? Could she bring down her walls and expose herself to pain yet again? "Chase, you can't always get what you want."

"I used to believe that. Not anymore. I love you. Please don't walk away from me again. Stay."

There were no guarantees. "Times change. What happens when it doesn't work out? When you get tired of me? When the challenge wears off?"

"Not going to happen."

She longed to believe him. "Chase…"

His brow creased and his lips thinned with determination. "I want forever. With you. That's where this is heading. I'm done dating. I've found what I was looking for."

"I need to think. I—"

He took her hand and pressed it to his heart. "We both analyze too much. It gets us in trouble. You don't need to think. For once, just feel."

The thump of his heartbeat reverberated beneath her palm.

"I love you," he said. "Tell me what it's going to take."

"Would you make me CEO?"

He laid his other hand atop hers. "Is that what you really want?"

No, it wasn't. She'd thrown it out there to see how

he'd react. "I want us not to fight. But I have to work. And I can't have you undercutting me. No more power plays."

"Equal footing."

She nodded and tears began to flow. "Yes. That would be nice."

"Shh." He drew her into his arms then. "Don't cry. It's all going to be good between us from here on out."

"I'm so scared."

He pulled her tighter. "I'll let you in on a secret—so am I. But do you love me like my grandfather says you do?"

"Yes." The word seemed to carry on the still air. "And it's hurt so badly. That's why I quit. I couldn't stay. Not loving you like this. You needed to be CEO more than I did."

"I need you more than I need to be CEO."

"It has to be a McDaniel on the letterhead," she said.

"It will be. But our life is more important." He lowered his head for a light kiss. "I'm going to make all your dreams come true. I love you. It'll be amazing what we can do, so long as we're together."

And in the stillness of the night, Miranda believed.

Epilogue

"You know, I'm getting tired of these impromptu board meetings," Walter Peters grumbled as he took his seat on Tuesday afternoon. He turned to Leroy. "Do you know what this is about?"

"Nope. Chase hasn't said a thing. Like I told you, he took off early Saturday morning and I haven't seen him since."

"I haven't heard from Miranda since this weekend, either. Do you think they ran into each other and fought?"

"I have no idea," Leroy replied. He and Walter had been over this several times already.

Kathleen Kennedy came into the room and glared at the two men. "If you have any more tricks up your sleeves, I'm going to resign," she warned.

"I'm at a loss, too," Leroy announced. He took inventory. A few people hadn't been able to drop everything and show, but the board had a majority present, which was all Chase needed. The agenda had been pretty vague, which wasn't acceptable at all. If he were running things, it'd be different.

His grandson finally entered the room, Carla on his heels. They left the door open.

"Thanks for coming," Chase said. "I have some important items we need to vote on. I've filled our corporate vacancies."

Leroy leaned back in his chair. His grandchildren still didn't like him being here, but the doctor said he was doing well, and he couldn't stand sitting at home. "We don't need to vote on that," he said.

"No, but you do need to vote on the restructuring of McDaniel Manufacturing."

"Again?" Kathleen asked. She scowled at Leroy. "Your family is giving me gray hair."

It was Chase who answered. "Yes, again. Most companies have a chief executive officer and a company president, each playing a vital role. Since my return I've reanalyzed our five-year growth plan, and it's in our best interests to make this change. We will maintain the vice president position and permanently fill it with Emily Feng."

"Do you have someone in mind for the role of company president?" Walter asked as Carla passed out folders containing detailed job descriptions and the new corporate structure.

"I do, but we need to approve the proposal first. The full specs are in front of you. Basically, the CEO is at the top, but the company president takes care of day-to-day operations and the CEO is in charge of long-range planning. Will someone make a motion?"

"Absolutely," Leroy said, and a minute later, the motion passed.

"Thank you," Chase said.

"So who is this person?" Walter asked.

Leroy leaned forward in his chair. He was certain he knew, but he had to see this for himself. As Miranda walked through the door, he felt tears prick his eyelids, and he banged his fist on the table. "Finally you got it right."

"Oh, I did." Chase reached around and drew Miranda to him. "I also hope you can all make it to the lake next summer for our wedding. We're hosting an engagement party next Saturday afternoon at Leroy's. I hope you don't mind. Your house is bigger."

Carla began to pass out invitations.

"Best thing you've ever done," Leroy said, trying to blink away the tears.

THE DAY LEROY TURNED eighty-one, he walked Miranda down the aisle, which was a long white runner in the meadow behind the lodge. "You sure you want to do this?" he teased.

"Absolutely," Miranda replied. The weather was perfect, and there, less than fifty feet away now, Chase stood waiting. He was so handsome in his tux, but the smile on his face and the light in his eyes were what drew her. Both showed how much he loved her.

A year ago, on her first trip to the lake, she hadn't known she could ever find this much joy. She and Chase had managed to work together successfully, as equals. By tomorrow it would be official—two McDaniels would run the company.

As Leroy and she approached, Miranda saw Chris place his hand on his brother's shoulder. While Chris would officiate, she and Chase had written their own vows.

She hoped she wouldn't cry. Already her sister, the maid of honor, was dabbing at her eyes.

Leroy stopped as Chase stepped forward. "Thank you for making me so happy," the older man said, giving her a kiss on the cheek. "You have it all."

Miranda reached for Chase's arm so he could walk her the rest of the way. Only two words fit at a time like this.

"I do."

* * * * *

The dark figures on the dock were still firing. The bullets cutting through the surface of the water without the warning boom of shots told Eve they were using silencers.

That was to her benefit. Silencers decreased the accuracy of every shot and lessened the range.

She grabbed for the rocks. Scrambled through the darkness. Bumped her knee on a boulder. Cursed.

Burrowing into the waist-deep grass, she kept low and crawled forward. Faster. Pushed harder. Needed as much distance as possible.

Shots pinged on the rocks.

J.T. scrambled alongside her.

He was breathing hard.

They had to stay close to the ground until they reached the next row of warehouses. Even though she was relatively certain they were out of range at this point, she wasn't taking any risks. And she wasn't slowing down.

J.T. had to keep up.

The splat of a bullet hitting the ground next to Eve had her rolling left. Maybe they weren't completely out of range.

She bumped J.T. He grunted.

His injured arm. Dammit. She could apologize later.

Half a dozen more yards.

Almost in the clear.

As she reached the cover of the alley between the first two warehouses she tensed.

Silence.

No pings or splats.

She glanced back at the dock. Deserted.

Time to run.

Her car was parked another block down.

Pushing to her feet, she sprinted forward. The wet bag dragged at her shoulder. She ignored it.

By the time she reached the lot where her car was parked, she had dug the keys from her pocket and hit the fob. Six seconds later she was behind the wheel. She hit the ignition as J.T. collapsed into the passenger seat. Tires squealed as she spun out of the slot.

"What the hell did you do to me?"

From the corner of her eye she watched him shake his head in an attempt to clear it.

He would be pissed when she told him about the tranquilizer.

She'd needed him cooperative until she formulated a plan. A drug-induced state of unconsciousness had been the fastest and most efficient method to ensure his continued solidarity.

"I can't really talk right now." Eve weaved into the right lane as the street widened to four lanes. What she needed was traffic. It was Saturday night—shouldn't be that difficult to find as soon as they were out of the old warehouse district.

A glance in the rearview mirror warned that their unwanted company had caught up.

Sensing her tension, J.T. turned to peer over his left shoulder.

"I hope you have a plan B."

She shot him a look. "There's always plan G." Then she pulled the Glock out of her waistband.

Cutting the steering wheel left, she slid between two vehicles. Another veer to the right and she'd put several cars between hers and the enemy.

She was betting they wouldn't pull out the firepower in the open like this, but a girl could never be too sure when it came to an unknown enemy.

Deep blending was the way to go.

Two traffic lights ahead the marquis of a movie theater provided exactly the opportunity she was looking for.

The digital numbers on the dash indicated it was just past midnight. Perfect timing. The late movie would be purging its audience into the crowd of teen-agers who liked hanging out in the parking lot.

She took a hard right onto the property that sported a twelve-screen theater, numerous fast-food hot spots and a chain superstore. Speeding across the lot, she selected a lane of parking slots. Pulling in as close to the theater entrance as possible, she shut off the engine and reached for her door.

"Let's go."

Thankfully he didn't argue.

Rounding the hood of her car, she shoved the Glock into her bag, then wrapped her arm around J.T.'s and merged into the crowd.

With her free hand she finger-combed her long hair. It was soaked, as were her clothes. The kids she bumped into noticed, gave her death-ray glares.

They just didn't know.

As she and J.T. moved in closer to the building, she grabbed a baseball cap from an innocent bystander. The crowd made it easy. The kid who owned the cap had made it even easier by stuffing the cap bill-first into his waistband at the small of his back.

Pushing through the loitering crowd, she made her way to the side of the building next to the main entrance. She pushed J.T. against the wall and dropped her bag to the ground. Peeled off her tee and let it fall.

His gaze instantly zeroed in on her breasts, where the cami she wore had glued to her skin like an extra layer. A zing of desire shot through her veins.

Not the time.

With a flick of her wrist she twisted her hair up and clamped the cap atop the blond mass.

"They're coming," J.T. muttered as he gazed at some point beyond her.

"Yeah, I know." She planted her palms against the wall on either side of him and leaned in. "Keep your eyes open. Let me know when they're inside."

Then she planted her lips on his.

* * * * *

Will J.T. and Eve be caught in the moment?
Or will Eve get the chance to reveal all of her
secrets?
Find out in
THE BRIDE'S SECRETS
by Debra Webb.
Available August 2009 from Harlequin Intrigue®.

We'll be spotlighting a different series every month throughout 2009 to celebrate our 60th anniversary.

LOOK FOR
HARLEQUIN INTRIGUE®
IN AUGUST!

To commemorate the event, Harlequin Intrigue® is thrilled to invite you to the wedding of the Colby Agency's J.T. Baxley and his bride, Eve Mattson.

Look for *Colby Agency: Elite Reconnaissance*

THE BRIDE'S SECRETS
BY DEBRA WEBB

Available August 2009

www.eHarlequin.com

HIBPA09

REQUEST YOUR FREE BOOKS!

2 FREE NOVELS PLUS 2
FREE GIFTS!

> *American ★ Romance®*

Love, Home & Happiness!

YES! Please send me 2 FREE Harlequin® American Romance® novels and my 2 FREE gifts (gifts are worth about $10). After receiving them, if I don't wish to receive any more books, I can return the shipping statement marked "cancel." If I don't cancel, I will receive 4 brand-new novels every month and be billed just $4.24 per book in the U.S. or $4.99 per book in Canada.* That's a savings of close to 15% off the cover price! It's quite a bargain! Shipping and handling is just 50¢ per book. I understand that accepting the 2 free books and gifts places me under no obligation to buy anything. I can always return a shipment and cancel at any time. Even if I never buy another book from Harlequin, the two free books and gifts are mine to keep forever.

154 HDN EYSE   354 HDN EYSQ

Name _____ (PLEASE PRINT) _____

Address _____ Apt. # _____

City _____ State/Prov. _____ Zip/Postal Code _____

Signature (if under 18, a parent or guardian must sign) _____

Mail to the **Harlequin Reader Service:**
IN U.S.A.: P.O. Box 1867, Buffalo, NY 14240-1867
IN CANADA: P.O. Box 609, Fort Erie, Ontario L2A 5X3

Not valid to current subscribers of Harlequin® American Romance® books.

Want to try two free books from another line?
Call 1-800-873-8635 or visit www.morefreebooks.com.

* Terms and prices subject to change without notice. Prices do not include applicable taxes. N.Y. residents add applicable sales tax. Canadian residents will be charged applicable provincial taxes and GST. Offer not valid in Quebec. This offer is limited to one order per household. All orders subject to approval. Credit or debit balances in a customer's account(s) may be offset by any other outstanding balance owed by or to the customer. Please allow 4 to 6 weeks for delivery. Offer available while quantities last.

Your Privacy: Harlequin is committed to protecting your privacy. Our Privacy Policy is available online at www.eHarlequin.com or upon request from the Reader Service. From time to time we make our lists of customers available to reputable third parties who may have a product or service of interest to you. If you would prefer we not share your name and address, please check here. ☐

HAR09R

You're invited to join our Tell Harlequin Reader Panel!

By joining our new reader panel you will:

- Receive Harlequin® books—they are FREE and yours to keep with no obligation to purchase anything!
- Participate in fun online surveys
- Exchange opinions and ideas with women just like you
- Have a say in our new book ideas and help us publish the best in women's fiction

In addition, you will have a chance to win great prizes and receive special gifts!
See Web site for details. Some conditions apply.
Space is limited.

To join, visit us at
www.TellHarlequin.com.

Welcome to the intensely emotional world of

MARGARET WAY

with

Cattle Baron: Nanny Needed

It's a media scandal! Flame-haired beauty
Amber Wyatt has gate-crashed her ex-fiancé's
glamorous society wedding. Groomsman
Cal McFarlane knows she's trouble, but when
Amber loses her job, the rugged cattle rancher
comes to the rescue. He needs a nanny, and
if it makes his baby nephew happy, he's
willing to play with fire….

*Available in August
wherever books are sold.*

HRI7601

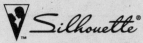

Silhouette®

Romantic
SUSPENSE

**Sparked by Danger,
Fueled by Passion.**

CAVANAUGH
JUSTICE

The Cavanaughs are back!

USA TODAY bestselling author

Marie Ferrarella

Cavanaugh Pride

In charge of searching for a serial killer on the loose,
Detective Frank McIntyre has his hands full. When
Detective Julianne White Bear arrives in town searching
for her missing cousin, Frank has to keep the escalating
danger under control while trying to deny the very
real attraction he has for Julianne. Can they keep their
growing feelings under wraps while also handling the
most dangerous case of their careers?

Available August wherever books are sold.

Visit Silhouette Books at www.eHarlequin.com

SRS27641

Harlequin® Historical
Historical Romantic Adventure!

From *USA TODAY* bestselling author
Margaret Moore

THE VISCOUNT'S KISS

When Lord Bromwell meets a young woman on the mail coach to Bath, he has no idea she is Lady Eleanor Springford—until *after* they have shared a soul-searing kiss!

The nature-mad viscount isn't known for his spontaneous outbursts of romance—and the situation isn't helped by the fact that the woman he is falling for is fleeing a forced marriage....

The Viscount and the Runaway...

Available August 2009
wherever you buy books.

HH29557

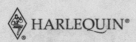

HARLEQUIN®

American ★ *Romance*®

COMING NEXT MONTH
Available August 11, 2009

#1269 THE RODEO RIDER by Roxann Delaney
Men Made in America
A vacation was all attorney Jules Vandeveer needed to clear her head. But rest was the last thing on her mind when she met rodeo rider Tanner O'Brien. Jules was immediately drawn to the rugged cowboy, and her heart went out to him and his rebellious nephew. Helping them heal wasn't a problem…but for once, walking away would be.

#1270 MISTLETOE MOMMY by Tanya Michaels
4 Seasons in Mistletoe
Dr. Adam Varner planned this trip to Mistletoe to reconnect with his kids. When he rescued a stranded pet sitter with car trouble, he didn't expect Brenna Pierce to have such an amazing connection with his daughters and son. Brenna is the woman Adam didn't know he was looking for—can he make a temporary stay in Mistletoe into something more…permanent?

#1271 SAMANTHA'S COWBOY by Marin Thomas
Samantha Cartwright needs to access her trust fund to start up a ranch for abused horses. Wade Dawson needs to keep Samantha distracted until he can figure out where her missing money went! So Wade spends as much time at Sam's ranch as he can—and, with Sam, discovers his inner cowboy….

#1272 ONE OF A KIND DAD by Daly Thompson
Fatherhood
Daniel Foster has built his own family looking after foster kids. And when he meets Lilah Ross and starts to fall for her, he knows he wants Lilah and her young son to be a part of that family, too. But when Lilah's ex-husband threatens her son, Daniel is afraid he could lose them both.

HARCNMBPA0709